Rita

Thank you ... reading!

Thank you for your
support and being a
great cousin
over the years.

Mma B

Because OF You

CHASING
OKLAHOMA

MELISSA ROBERTS

outskirts
press

Because of You
Chasing Oklahoma
All Rights Reserved.
Copyright © 2020 Melissa Roberts
v1.0

Outskirts Press, Inc.
http://www.outskirtspress.com

ISBN: 978-1-9772-2212-1

Library of Congress Control Number: 2020901043

PRINTED IN THE UNITED STATES OF AMERICA

*E*ventually my story will be told.

Sitting on a ridge just before sunrise, I tossed back my long, dark hair. It was a chilly, clear morning. Tears were falling down my cheeks as I cried tears of fear and joy, unsure of which emotion I should be feeling, torn between doing what was right for me or doing what was right for everyone else. This was an unconventional love affair—certainly not one you encounter every day, but one so crafted by love that it would leave a permanent void deep down inside your soul for years to come.

This void is my reality. I will be never be strong enough to change it.

The mist from the salty air covered my face and neck. My name is Taylor and I am about to tell you the saddest or most incredible love story that you have ever heard. The choice will be yours to make. A life of secrets and hiding that will span three decades. This is where my story begins and likely where it will end. I'm still not sure if I hate myself or love myself more for the decisions that I have made. I know that I cannot change the past, and I have been completely unable to change the future. Love is a powerful force, and we don't always choose love. Love often chooses us.

Chapter One

THE MORNING AFTER

SHAWN:

I woke up at 5:30 a.m. to the sound of doors slamming and people shouting in the hotel parking lot. Looking around the room, there was no sign of her. Sitting up on the side of the king-sized bed, I found only a note that she had written—a note that was not in ink, but rather, a dark shade of red lipstick. Not sure of which emotion I should be feeling at the time, I plowed straight into anger mode. No name and no number was left. She clearly wanted to leave only the beautiful memory that we shared the last two nights.

Knowing very little about her, I shot into action to try every way I could to find her. This was not my town and not my people. The only things I knew about her were that she was beautiful, possibly in college, and drove a red Mustang convertible. I was a struggling music man with secrets and demons of my own.

Long before the internet, finding things out about someone was extremely difficult. It took perseverance and determination to gain the smallest piece of knowledge. After getting dressed and rooting through everything left in the hotel room hoping to find the smallest of clues, I left the room full of only memories behind.

My friend John asked, "Shawn, did you happen to catch her name?"

"No, man, I did not."

"You spent two nights with this girl and never asked her name? What the hell is wrong with you?"

John and I have been friends since high school. We often played music together. Bar after bar, night after night. It was totally out of character for me to hook up with some random girl. She was different somehow. I couldn't get her off of my mind

Days later, John and a couple of buddies of mine were having a drink. Sam pulled out a picture he had taken of a car a few nights ago that he really loved. It was a red Mustang. He told John that he saw me leave the bar in that car with a girl in it. John jerked the pictures from his hand. With complete shock on my face, I asked to keep the pictures. One of them had the tag of the car in clear sight. It was just the ammunition I needed to get the name of the mysterious girl that drove away that night, leaving no trace of who she was.

Later that night, John told me about the tag on the back of the car. It was my only chance of possibly finding out anything about her. I had to find out who she was. I could still smell her perfume on my jacket. Her eyes twinkled every time she looked at me. I knew she was younger than me only by the way she made love to me. Her inexperience was tantalizing yet seductive.

I could not get her off of my mind. The days were so long. I worked a full-time job during the day and played music at night. Visions of her haunted me. Day and night, I could not concentrate. I vaguely remembered things about her. She had a tattoo on her lower back, the words "Don't die with dreams, die with memories" with a paper-thin line between them. Just below her belly button, to the right, was another one. It was a Celtic cross seductively tucked below her panty line. A belly button ring which fell just above her jeans. These were the things

2

that I remembered. My memories were fading fast. She drove away with my heart that morning.

I can't breathe most days. God knows that I have tried to get her out of my mind. Guilt and regret are the two hardest things to live with. Most people have to live with one or the other. I had to live with both.

Chapter Two

DEALING WITH DONNA

❧

TAYLOR:

The long days and long nights were killing me. Day after day, trying to juggle school and work was exhausting. I worked full time in a nightclub. Being very shy, I never made many friends. I had my handful of those that I could always depend on—only a few that I really trusted. Trust was never my strong suit. I was more of a suffer in silence kind of girl. A runner when it came to relationships.

Kerrie was my best friend at the time. She and I talked about everything. She was the first to notice that something was bothering me. Donna was also part of our tribe. We all stuck together. Tightly woven like silk fabric. Beautiful yet fragile. Donna worked with me at the club. Our stage names were Sunshine and Rain. We mixed well together. By the end of most nights, the money was rolling in. Despite our exhaustion, our focus was on making as much money as we could.

Kerrie was never much into the bar scene. She worked most nights waiting tables at Hooters. It worked for her. She was a kind but old soul, a great listener who never judged you no matter what. Often, it was Kerrie who picked up the broken pieces of my heart. She was my angel of stability and love. Life was never easy for us, but we made the most of it.

"Taylor!"

A strong, firm shake on my shoulder woke me up from a deep sleep. I felt exhausted after my shift, so I decided to lie down on the sofa in the break room of the bar. It was damp and smoky in there, but I was used to it.

Donna gazed at me with deep concern.

"What has been up with you lately?" she yelled. "You walk the floors all night. You always look tired. Are you pregnant?"

"No!" I exclaimed. "I just have a lot on my mind."

"Do you want to talk about it?" Donna pressed on and on. Getting the feeling that she was not going to give in, I offered to talk if we could leave and talk over drinks. Drinks. That always makes talking easier. A truth serum. Feeling vulnerable already, I knew I needed to drown my emotions a little before I could speak freely. I knew I would be judged and completely dismissed once Donna got wind that this not only involved a guy but a two-night stand.

"A two-night stand? Taylor, you totally broke the number one rule when hooking up with a guy. Never stay overnight, and never ever give him your real name. Did you tell him your real name?"

"No!" I responded with a deep sigh. "That's the problem. I have so many regrets. I cannot get him out of my mind. I can't sleep and I can hardly eat. Every moment of the day is consumed with the faint memory of his face. I'm dying inside. Donna, I really need your support right now. I feel like my heart has been shattered into a million pieces."

"Seriously, Taylor?" Donna exclaimed. "I can't believe you let yourself get so wrapped up in this guy after only two nights. I've had Tootsie Pops that lasted longer."

Laughing hysterically at me, Donna finally realized the depth of my emotions as I sat sobbing quietly with my head down on the table.

"I left the room early on the second morning purposely so that I did not need to converse with him. I only left a short note thanking him for the amazing night we shared together. I don't know his name or where he is from. I don't know why I can't get him off of my mind. I left a part of me there that morning in that hotel room. A part that I may never get back."

"We can do this together, Taylor," Donna said. "I'm heartbroken just listening to you. I will help you in any way I can. Tell me what you remember about him. Give me every piece of information that you have."

"That's the problem. I just don't have any information to offer...I will brainstorm and try to remember as much as I can."

Chapter Three

EXPLAINING TO KERRIE

was awakened by the heavy knocking at the door of my apartment. Kerrie was yelling hysterically my name....

"Taylor! Taylor! Are you in there?"

I stumbled out of bed, realizing that I had slept through my alarm.

"Oh my God!! What the hell...what time is it?"

"It's 10:30! You have slept through two of your classes."

Digging through my half-empty drawers and my overfilled closet, I pulled out random articles of clothing and put them on. The smell of a cigarette filled the room as Kerrie lit one up in an effort to calm herself down.

"Taylor, I thought something happened to you. Donna filled me in on the guy that you have been upset over, and I figured this may have something to do with him."

"The guy? Are you kidding me right now, Kerrie? You know me better than that. So much for me asking Donna to keep it silent for now. I guess we all know who we can trust."

"Oh Taylor, don't get mad at Donna. She was genuinely concerned about you. So am I. You have been acting strange for two weeks. You look anorexic, and you're always late. Does he have something to do with all of this? Are you pregnant?"

"Why does everyone keep asking me that?" I yelled. "No, I am not pregnant. I am over it and I don't want to talk about it anymore."

"Okay, but you know that I love you, right? You know you can come to me with anything. Day or night, I am always here for you."

That's what I have always loved about Kerrie. She doesn't hover. She is openly and unapologetically empathetic, but she also knows when to give you space. We have been friends for many years, and she knows me better than anyone.

I feel terrible that I lied to her. I am not okay. My grades are crashing, and I'm drinking almost every night. I have called out of work at the club two nights this week. Bills are coming due, and I have no way to pay them.

I can't help but wonder if this guy has spent one second thinking about me. Part of me thinks this is the norm for him—bar scenes and different girls every weekend. Likely it was his routine, but I just could not let it go. I needed to find out for myself.

SHAWN

SHAWN:

*I*t was a hot, humid day in the South. Sweat was pouring down my back. I was emotionally and physically drained. My wife was at home with our kids and I was thinking about someone I didn't even know and would likely never meet, every second of the day. I couldn't sleep, most nights. Every weekend, I scoured the crowds in the club, hoping she would return.

"Shawn, do you want to go out for a beer after work?"

John was nightly drinking buddy of mine. He and I had been friends since high school. He also played in the band with me. We called ourselves The Backwoods Boys—just a few country boys with a love of music, hoping to make it big someday. We worked in oil fields during the day and played music on the weekends. John used to be married but now he had only himself to take care of. I married very young and had children very soon after. I never regretted that decision. I do now question it. If I really loved my family, then why was I thinking about a girl that I knew nothing about? It haunted me. That night was the first time that I stepped out on my marriage.

I was exhausted and ready to head to the bar for a cold one with John. It was at least a hundred degrees in the field today.

Sitting at a tall table the cool air had a calming effect on us both. The bar was thick with smoke, and the smell of spilled beer permeated the walls.

"Shawn, I know you have had a hard time lately. I am worried about you. Is everything okay at home? Are you and Nicole having problems?"

JOHN:

*R*unning his hands through his thick, dirty-blond hair, Shawn hesitated to answer. I had to either let it go or press on. Shawn had not been himself. He was late for work almost every day and always seemed tired within the first hour. His brother committed suicide a few months back, and I wondered if that might have something to do with his acting so strangely.

"I am here for you, buddy, if you ever want to talk," I said.

"I'm okay," Shawn said in a low, unconvincing voice. "I just have a lot on my mind lately."

A few drinks in, Shawn decided to open up and talk about what he was feeling— extreme guilt for cheating yet extreme sadness for not making a connection with the girl that he could not seem to get off of his mind.

I could tell this was weighing heavily on Shawn's mind. I was torn about the decision to tell him or not tell him that I asked a police officer and buddy of mine to run the tag and get her information. I knew everything about her—where she lived, where went to college, and what her name was. I was literally stalking her. I questioned my decision to discuss this with him. I was close to him and Nicole as a family and knew the impact infidelity would have on their marriage. I held this information back for a bit because I really thought his feelings for this girl would blow over. I was terribly wrong.

"Where are we playing at this weekend, brother?"

Shawn replied after a long sigh.

"The Old Ranch. I really love that place. It was the first place that I ever played my songs. I have deep respect for the people there. They have always been good to me. My grandmother used to work there."

I laughed in a cocky sort of way. "I bet she did! She was a looker in her heyday."

Shawn said, "My grandma lit a fire in me at a young age to sing and play the guitar. It was in my blood."

"Let's have a few more and then call it a night. We have an early morning and we can't be late," I said.

Shawn laughed under his breath, knowing that comment was definitely directed at him.

The car ride home seemed to take forever. Hardly two words were spoken between us. Somehow I knew I needed to tell Shawn that I had this information. A part of me wanted to tell him tonight and another part wanted to wait a while. I struggled with the decision that would possibly change Shawn's life forever.

As I got out of the car, I thanked him for the ride. I walked away and left him with a deep thought.

"If there was anything you could change or do different in your life, what would it be?"

Shawn replied after a few seconds of thought, "I will get back to you on that."

"Fair enough, buddy. But I needed to leave you with something." We both laughed and called it a night.

Chapter Five

THE ENVELOPE

⸻

$\mathcal{J}$ ohn walked into the break room at lunch after sweating all morning working in the heat. I was sitting slumped over the table eating what Nicole had lovingly packed for me this morning. John slammed down a large manila envelope onto the table.

"Do with it what you want!"

"What?" I said.

John turned around and left the break room. I couldn't imagine what was so important that John would make such a big deal over. I leaned over and picked up the envelope. On the opposite side John had written a short note.

Shawn,

We have been friends a long time. I struggled with the decision to give you this information or simply hold on to it in hopes that someday you would no longer need it. What is written in here could change your life forever. Either way, I did what I felt in my heart that I needed to do. I love Nicole and I have always been envious of you and your family, likely because I was never fortunate enough to have one. Make whatever decision you feel is right for you. I will always be here for you, brother, and I will support any decision that you make.

Love, John

Tears filled my eyes and I read the note twice. I was curious about what was inside, but I also cautiously made the decision to wait and think it through before opening it. A million possibilities rolled through my mind. I turned to walk away when it hit me like a freight train. *He knows who she is.* My heart sank to the floor.

Later that day as I was clocking out, I saw John waiting in the hall for me. We were both hot and worn out from a hard day of work, and yet we always felt we were good enough for an evening drink together before heading home. The ride over together was quiet. The manila envelope was sitting in the seat between us. I could tell John was really looking at it, trying to see if I had opened it or not. My cell phone rang. I looked down and saw that it was Nicole. I was in no place to answer right now.

"Aren't you going to answer that?" John asked in a concerned voice.

"No, I am not. Not right now. I just can't deal with whatever issue she has with me right now. I have lost my will to fight with her anymore. Every day it's something new, and the distance between us is widening."

"Does it have anything to do with Taylor?"

"Taylor?" I exclaimed. "Who is Taylor?"

"Well, I guess you haven't opened the envelope yet."

"How did you find out her name? Are you absolutely sure that it is her?"

"I am positive, Shawn. I had a friend of mine run her tag. In that envelope you will find much more. I told you that if you pursue this, it could change your life forever."

Pulling into the bar, I was a bag of mixed emotions. I needed a drink now more than ever. We sat around and drank for hours. Drink after drink.

"I think Nicole senses my distance and that's why she is so upset lately. I just can't pull my shit together, man. This is so out of character for me."

JOHN:

*S*hawn's cheeks were red and his thick curly hair was laden with sweat. One drink after another was certainly not helping the situation.

"I think we should call it a night," I said. "Let me drive us home tonight. I will pick you up tomorrow morning for work. I am sure Nicole is worried sick about you. Oh, and I think I will hold on to this envelope until you are sure you want it."

Silence filled the air on the long ride home. Shawn was dangling his arm out of the window as if he were trying to catch fireflies. We used to do that when we were young. Catch fireflies and put them in a jar for safekeeping, only to find them dead the next day for a lack of air. Ironic, isn't it? Saving something for safekeeping? Sometimes saving for safekeeping only eats us up inside and corrodes our emotions like a sea wall after a storm. I'm glad that I gave the information to Shawn. I could see the storm troubling his soul and corroding his every emotion. The only thing left to do was wait. I did not know which way he would go, but I felt confident this was a path he needed to explore.

Chapter Six

NICOLE

I was sitting in the living room crying on the couch when I heard the door open. I could tell he was trying to be quiet so that he could sneak in unnoticed to avoid a fight.

"Where have you been, Shawn? It's two in the morning and you are usually home by midnight. Was John with you?"

"Yes, he just dropped me off. I drank too much to drive tonight and definitely too much to stay up and argue with you. I'm going to bed."

I followed him down the hall and into the bathroom. He pulled out his toothbrush and started brushing his teeth.

"I'm serious, Shawn. What is it going to take to get you to tell me what is wrong? Is it something I did wrong? If I did something, please, let's talk about it."

"It's two in the morning, Nicole! I just don't have it in me tonight. Let's talk about it another time. I'm okay, I just have a lot on my mind. I need to do better for you and the kids. I need to do better for myself. I'm writing my music and singing in bars from coast to coast and I am still getting nowhere . I work my ass off day after day in the field and getting nowhere. Do you get the picture now? Please, I just want to go to bed. It's not you. It's me, but I will work it out. I love you, Nicole, with all of my heart. Please don't question that. I'm going to bed now."

He kissed me on the forehead and went to bed. I stayed up the rest of the night crying and wondering if my biggest fear was about to come true. Was Shawn having an affair? Could this be what would break our family apart? I knew deep down inside that even if I found out he was, I would have to let it go—overlook the obvious and keep our family together.

Morning came so quick. The kids were up, and I was making breakfast. I looked over at the clock on the wall and realized Shawn was going to be late for work. I ran upstairs and down the hall to wake him. He was up already and putting his shoes on.

"Aren't you going to eat?" I asked him, my voice trembling.

"I really don't have time, Nicole. I overslept and John will be here soon to pick me up."

"Can we talk tonight? I really want to make things better for us, but I can't without your help."

"I can't tonight. It's Friday, and we have a gig tonight down at the bar. The boys and I will head over there right after work to have drinks and set up. Don't wait up for me. I will be home late."

He kissed me on the forehead, and out the door he went. His shirt was wrinkled and half tucked in. My eyes were filled with tears as I realized this was going to be the new normal in my life. My husband was chasing his dream, and I was chasing a hopeless marriage.

TAYLOR

I was lying in bed staring up at the ceiling when the loud bang on the door made me jump to my feet. I ran as quickly as I could for the door.

"Who is it?"

"It's me, Donna."

I unlocked the door and let her in. She quickly hugged me and kissed each side of my cheek.

"What's been going on with you, my friend? I haven't seen you in a while."

"Oh, I'm okay, I guess."

"You seem distant, Taylor. Kerrie and I are worried about you. Let's have a sugar night out!"

"No! Nope!" I exclaimed.

"Yes! It will be fun. Throw on a pair of shorts and flip-flops, and let's go. Sugary treats and chocolate milk always make everything better."

I turned around, shrugging my shoulders and rolling my eyes. I knew I wasn't going to win this one, so I got dressed and off we went.

Our favorite place to go when we had drama in our lives was Krispy Kreme Donut Shop. It was a plus if the red light was on and the donuts were hot. Oh, the smell was hypnotic. Soon I had no regrets about getting dressed and getting out of bed. We bought a dozen and two bottles of chocolate milk and off we went.

There were benches up and down Westshore Boulevard, but we had our favorite. Westshore was a beautiful area. It was a well-groomed, paved trail on the bay. Lights from the nearby downtown buildings twinkled off the water. We always chose the bench about halfway down the trail. It faced Tampa General Hospital where I was getting ready to start an internship. We planted our rumps there and opened up the box of donuts and began to talk. It was surprising, but actually as it turned out, glazed donuts were a far better truth serum than alcohol. I threw a couple back and downed some creamy chocolate milk, and I was geared up for battle. I was an emotional wreck right now, so emotional eating went with the territory.

"Are you ready?"

"I'm ready!"

"Tell me what's been going on in your life."

"Well," I sighed, as I forced myself to swallow. "I am a wreck, a disaster, and a hopeless mess."

"What the hell is going on, Taylor? I have never seen you like this."

"I know. I have never felt like this."

"Is this about Mr. Bar Guy?"

"Yes," I said, as I could no longer fight the tears that were rolling down my face. "I just don't know what to do. I just can't seem to let him go. Everything inside me longs to know him more. I know that I am being foolish. Let's face it; he probably picks up girls all the time and never thinks twice about it. Unlike him, I was young and innocent. I had never been with a guy before, and I think this is why it's been so hard for me."

Donna took a long pause before speaking. I wasn't sure if she was disapproving of my reaction or if she was searching for the right words to say. We had a few moments of silence. She looked at me with a straight face and said, "We really should have bought more donuts!"

I busted into an uncontrollable laugh. Boy, I really needed that. The tears shut off like a faucet, and we continued to laugh at ourselves for a good fifteen minutes. It was a much- needed break for me.

"Taylor, I can't say that I understand what you must be feeling right now. I am and will always be here for you. My advice really should mean very little. I only want it to serve as a small beacon of light in an otherwise stormy night on the ocean. I think we should try to find him."

"What if he rejects me?"

"He won't. Taylor, are you kidding me? And if he does, then it's his terrible loss. He can regret it the rest of his life. You shouldn't have to. I really think you need this closure. You are getting ready to start medical school and you don't need this hanging over our head or your heart."

I stared for a moment at Donna. "You are right. I have to try to find him. How do we go about doing it? Do you have any ideas?"

"Let me think. Do you remember the name of the bar that you were in or the name of the band?"

"Yes, I think they called themselves the Backwoods Boys or Backwoods Band. I can't remember which."

"I think that's a really good place to start."

"He was the lead singer, but he also played the guitar. The name of the bar escapes me right now."

"That's more information than I expected you to have. I think we can definitely find him. I just want your promise that no matter which way this goes, you will get through it. Just don't go in with expectations. Stay focused on closure. Can you do that?"

"I can! Donna, you are the best friend that I could ever hope for and I feel so undeserving of you. I'm crying again, but I'm not sure if I am happy or sad."

We stood up from the bench and hugged each other tightly. "I love you, Taylor, and I am so glad that you allowed me into your heart to help."

Empty milk bottles and an empty donut box were all that remained.

"Let's clean up this mess and head home, shall we?"

"Let's do!"

Donna dropped me off at my house close to midnight. I had a special place in my home where I liked to sit and do my best thinking. A lot of time had been spent there through the years. It was a wide windowsill that faced east—a perfect place to reflect under the stars but also the perfect place to watch the sunrise in the morning. That's exactly what I did. I never went to sleep that night. I had a million things going through my mind. I felt fear but was hopeful that I could find peace in whatever form it was going to come in. I knew I needed to brace myself for the worst-case scenario. I also knew that we made an incredible connection that night. I wished I had left things differently that morning. If I had left my number and he never called, then that would just make him a jerk. I could live with that. I also thought that somehow he would have called me if he could and we could talk and possibly meet up again. A million possibilities rocked mind that night. I stared outside at the stars for hours. The bushes in front of my window were fragrant and full of fireflies—my favorite summer show.

Chapter Eight

SHAWN OPENS
THE ENVELOPE

The bar was full and alive tonight. The guys and I always drew a large crowd. I sang the songs that everyone wanted to hear. I also always threw in one or two new ones that I had written just to get them out there. It was obvious that the people loved my work. I was booked out nearly a year every weekend, from the East Coast to the West Coast. The boys and I were broke and we never traveled in style, but we made it work. We hated being away from our families, but we pressed on, hoping someday for the big break we needed. We had interview after interview with multiple radio stations with little acknowledgment. Still, we continued on. Deep down inside, I really didn't mind being away from home. I missed my kids terribly, but I dreaded going home to face my wife every week. I knew that it was unfair for her. I also knew that I was struggling inside and fighting with my heart on a daily basis. The struggle was real, and I had to battle it alone.

John gave me the tools I needed, but I knew in my heart that I needed to leave him out of it. He was more than a friend. He was family, like a brother to me, and I felt so guilty letting him down. I knew I was not the man he thought I was. I never would be, but I still loved him and I knew that although I would disappoint him, he would not love me less.

Later that night after we played, John and I sat down at the bar and I told him that I planned to open the envelope tonight after we left the bar. I had thought about it and I was ready to move forward.

"Are you sure that you are ready?" John asked in an almost surprised voice.

"I am, brother. I have battled with this demon for way too long. I can't fight it anymore. It is destroying me inside. Hell, she may reject me and leave me crying out in the rain."

We both needed that laugh. . . .

I said, "I think it was obvious when she didn't leave her number that she didn't want to be contacted. I have to take the chance. I know the feeling of rejection. I also know the feeling of hopelessly wanting to be with someone and not being able to. I have to at least try. I just want you to know how thankful I am that you got the information for me. I will forever be grateful. I also don't want you to be put in the middle, so for that reason I won't mention this again to you unless you ask me."

"You know I will always be here for you, Shawn, so if you need me, please feel like you can reach out. I am here for you no matter what."

That night after leaving the bar, I parked on a side road and opened the envelope. I read her name out loud three times in disbelief. How could I have such an amazing two nights with this girl and never ask her name? Was I really that shallow? I would like to just think that I was lost in the moment. Had she asked my name? I struggled to remember. Okay, I was ready. I just realized how difficult this could end up being. She lived in Florida. Not even close to here. I figured she was a city girl. Would she ever really be happy in Oklahoma? It's hot as hell here and the storms are wicked. College girl. I dropped out of high school. This was not looking like the outcome I was hoping to get. I wondered if I would ever measure up to her expectations. The thought occurred to me—should I leave Nicole and then pursue Taylor, or should I find out if Taylor had any interest in me first? Either way, I was a jerk. I could barely make ends meet. I worked hard during the week and I was in bars every weekend. I stared up at the sky, holding her phone number in my hand. I needed a sign. A clear sign. I just needed to know.

The next day I called in to work but left the house anyway. I drove to a nearby hotel and checked in. I needed a quiet place to gather my thoughts and move forward with trying to contact her. It took three cups of coffee and a lot of rehearsing in front of the mirror before I could place the call. Finally, I picked up the phone and I dialed the number. She answered on the second ring.

"Hello?"

I paused. I couldn't speak, so I hung up the phone. I was sweating bullets. I ran my fingers through my hair so I could get the moisture away from my eyes. I dialed again. This time I could tell that she picked up the phone, but she didn't say hello. She waited for me to speak first.

"Hello, is this Taylor?"

"Yes, it is. Who is speaking?"

"This is Shawn. I am sorry to call you out of the blue like this, but I can't get you off of my mind."

Taylor was silent. I could tell that she had started crying.

"Taylor?"

"I'm here. I have been dying inside. I have so many regrets about leaving that morning without talking to you."

My heart was beating so fast that I had to sit down.

"I think about you all the time. My life has been a broken mess since I left your side that morning."

"Taylor, I feel the same way. I can't get you off of my mind. My whole life has been a mess. My job, my friends, and my family."

"It's so good to finally hear your voice again."

"When can I see you?"

"I also discovered a few fun facts about you."

"Really?" Taylor said in a concerned tone.

"Well, I found out that you live in Florida and I live in Oklahoma." We both laughed.

"It's just distance," Taylor said. "That, we can work around."

We planned to meet at the end of the month. The band had a gig in Nashville and Taylor agreed to drive up for the weekend. It was the beginning of something tragically beautiful.

Chapter Nine

TAYLOR SHARES THE NEWS

I could hardly wait to go to work that night. For the first time in months, I finally had a good night's sleep. My mind was rested, and a huge weight was lifted from my heart.

I walked into the club and Donna was the first to greet me. We were not going to open for another two hours, but the girls always came early to drink and dress before their shift started.

"What can I pour for you?" Donna said in a happy voice.

"I will have a shot of vodka, please."

"What is up with you, my friend? Wow! You look amazing!"

"I feel amazing! Donna, he found me! He contacted me, and we are going to meet at the end of the month. I am so excited. I slept so good last night, too!"

"This is big, Taylor!"

"How long did you talk to him? What did you find out about him? How in the world did he find you?"

"Okay, one question at a time. Well, I know he lives in Oklahoma. That's really about it. He and his band are playing at a bar in Nashville at the end of the month, and I am going to meet him there. I suppose I will find out more then. I am hopeful that we can find a way. Long distance is so hard. I was thinking that I could find a school near him to apply to. What are your thoughts on that?" I could see disapproval all over Donna's face.

"My thoughts? Are you sure you want my thoughts? First of all, I think you are nuts! What's in Oklahoma for you? Just him! Is that gonna be enough to keep you happy? You don't even know him yet, and you are already preparing to move near him. I think you should really get to know him better before you make the decision to do that. What does he do for a living? Is he in school somewhere?"

"Well, I know he plays music in a bar. He writes his own songs and he is very good. Amazing, actually."

"But does he have a real job?"

Donna was getting a bit anxious and I could hear it in her voice. Her cheeks were turning red and her forehead was blotchy.

"I don't know much more right now, Donna, but I am just excited to get to know him better."

Things continued to be tense, so I decided it was best to head on backstage and get dolled up to make some cash tonight.

The club was full of businessmen all coming in to catch a great show and drop some cash. Often, Donna and I would dance together. We each had a stage name. I was Sunshine and she was Rain. We complemented each other when we danced together. It was a Friday night and we always made a lot of money. Tonight, I was feeling especially playful, so I wore a cheetah outfit with a black thong underneath. I usually started with an outfit and stripteased onstage. That seemed to get me extra cash on any night.

It was never my intention to dance in a club for money, and I didn't plan on it long term. The schedule worked well with school, and the cash was really good. Donna's dad always helped us out when he could with our finances. He did not approve of the lifestyle that we had, but he chose to ignore it to avoid hard feelings.

Our shift tonight went by fast. The bar was closing, and Donna and I were cashing out our tips.

"Taylor, I don't want you to be upset by my negativity in this. I know this is what you need. I was thinking more closure than changing your whole life for this guy. I thought about it tonight and I really think I am so passionate about this because deep inside I'm angry and jealous at the same time. I am angry because if this works out for you, that means you will relocate and leave me here alone. You are my ride or die girl, and that thought is tearing me up inside. I am jealous because I have never known that kind of love—the kind that keeps you up at night and makes you do crazy things like move across the map to be with each other. I also don't want to see you hurt if this turns out to be a disaster. It could go either way, but just know that I will support you through this. I will try to be more supportive and less negative."

"Donna, thank you for your kind words. I really, really need support right now. I don't know if I am doing the right thing, but I at least have to try. I don't want to lose us in the process. I need you now more than ever. Ride or die!"

Chapter Ten

TAYLOR GOES TO NASHVILLE

───── ❧ ─────

*I*t was the longest month of my life, but it was finally time to head to Nashville. I was full of excitement and fear all at the same time. My mind felt like a tornado was hitting it. I was a whirlwind of emotions. We had spoken very little over the past month. It seemed he was only available late at night. I worked nights, so that made our time very limited. By the time I arrived, they would already be playing music in the bar. I wondered if he would recognize me. I was so excited to see him. My heart was skipping beats, and I felt short of breath.

SHAWN:

*I*could barely concentrate on playing music tonight. Every five seconds, I was looking at the door. Anytime now, she was going to walk through it. Part of me felt sick from being nervous, and the other part was jumping with excitement. I wondered how I should approach her. I broke my drinking rule tonight. I try not to drink when I play music because I usually can't stop and I end up drunk onstage. The crowd seems to like it, but I feel like my performance drags. Tonight I had to make an exception. My nerves could not take it without a little bit of liquid courage. John and Sam were oblivious to the situation. I did not tell anyone about her coming tonight.

I saw her the moment she walked into the bar. She was exactly as I remembered. A calm spread throughout me. It was a weird feeling. I made eye contact with her and I smiled. I turned back to look at John to see if he noticed. He smiled back at me and shook his head. I could tell he was happy for me, though he would never say it.

My heart wanted me to run to her and hug her. I had felt so disconnected since she left me that morning months ago. I could not wait for a break.

TAYLOR:

I was sitting at a high-top table near the bar. It was slightly smoky and very loud, but I couldn't have been happier. I shot Donna a text to let her know that I had arrived.

"He is on stage and he is looking mighty fine!"

I was tossing back one drink after another. The light started turning up and the music switched to a DJ as the band announced a break. My heart was beating so fast that I felt like I couldn't breathe. I looked up and he was walking straight toward me. We made eye contact and immediately I jumped up and ran to his arms. We embraced for what felt like forever. I felt like I was going to cry and I was fighting to hold back the tears. He softly whispered hello in my ear. I whispered it back.

"Taylor!" Shawn said with a hint of excitement in his voice. "It is so nice to finally see you again. When you left that morning, you took half of my heart with you, and I had to get it back."

Hearing those words made tears fall down my face.

"I am truly sorry, Shawn, for leaving the way I did. I thought that was what we both wanted, but I quickly realized that it was a huge mistake—one that I had no clue how to fix. How in the world did you find me?"

"John found you! I shared with him in confidence that I was struggling inside since you left me with no contact information. Apparently someone took multiple photos of your car that night and your tag was clearly legible in one of the pictures. He has a buddy in law enforcement, and that is how he got your information. I struggled inside trying to figure out if I should contact you or not. I couldn't fight the demons, so I decided to call. I'm glad I did. I wouldn't trade this moment for anything in this world."

We held eye contact for several seconds. Then he said, "Baby, we gotta hit the stage again for a couple of hours. After that, I am all yours!"

I sat there the next two hours fidgeting with excitement. My mind was wandering in so many different directions. I couldn't tell you any of the songs that they were singing, because I was in a better place. I kept thinking about the last time we were together. It all started in a bar just like this one. The next couple of days after we met were the best days of my life. He totally rocked my world.

Every time he made eye contact, he would smile. My heart would just melt. He had an adorable smile—well-defined dimples on his cheeks and the most beautiful eyes I have ever seen on a man. They were a blue-green color. His hair was longer than I remembered—dirty-blond and very curly. I kept looking at my watch. I knew I needed to slow down the drinking. The last thing that I wanted was to be drunk and not remember how amazing tonight was going to be.

Finally! Yes! The band was finished. He walked off the stage and grabbed my hand, and we both ran out a side door. As soon as the door closed behind us, he lifted me off the ground and we embraced in the most amazing kiss. I just melted in his arms. My entire body felt limp. It just really felt right.

"I just can't believe this is really happening, Shawn."

He put me back down on the ground.

"Hey baby, are you hungry? Do you want to go out, or would you rather just go back to the room where we can be alone and talk?"

I hesitated to make the decision. Was there a right or wrong answer here? My heart really just wanted to be alone with him. I just said it without hesitation. "I really would like to be alone. Our time is so limited, and I want to really get to know you."

"I feel the same way!" Shawn said without hesitation. "Let's go to the room."

We arrived at the room. It was an average room. No bells or whistles. As soon as we got in and comfortable, he poured us both a drink. Deep down, I really just wanted to jump in the bed with him—play now and talk later. His mind was not on the same thing, obviously, because he immediately shut that thought down.

"Taylor, before we go any further, there is something I have to tell you. There is no right time or right way to do this, but it has to be done. These last few months have been a total nightmare for me. I struggled with my demons every day, but I could not get you off of my mind. I really feel like I am in love with you, but how can I be?"

"Shawn, I feel the same way." I came closer to him to embrace him with a kiss. He gently pushed me away.

"Taylor, I have to be honest with you, and I can only pray to God that you will have an open mind and not run out the door. I am married."

Total silence filled the room.

"I also have two children."

I just stood there frozen with emotion. Tears were rolling down my face. "Shawn, how could you?"

"Taylor, I never meant for any of this to happen. A one-night stand was totally out of character for me, much less a two-night stand. I tried to forget about you. I tried to forget everything that happened that night, but I just couldn't. I have so much fear inside. I am so afraid that you are going to walk out that door and I will never see you again."

31

I sat on the end of the bed, crying, with my head in my hands.

"Taylor, please say something?"

"How could you do this to me, Shawn? How could you do this to your family? Your kids? I really thought we had something real!"

"We do, Taylor! If this wasn't real, I would have never made the effort to find you. I have not slept a full night since the morning that you left. Please don't leave me, Taylor. Not now. Please give me a chance to figure this out and try to make things right between us."

Silence once again filled the room.

"Shawn, I don't want to leave. I have struggled with this, too. I couldn't get you out of my head. I just don't know how we can do this."

Shawn grabbed me and pulled me to him. He gently unzipped my short black dress and it fell to the floor. He picked me up and carried me over to the bed and he took his clothes off piece by piece. He never broke eye contact with me. He gently embraced me and started kissing me all over. We made love several times that night. It was the most amazing night that I have ever spent with a man. We eventually fell asleep. I woke up early but I just lay beside him. I couldn't bear the thought of losing him. I also could not imagine him leaving his wife and kids for me. Kids! My heart was torn into so many pieces. What I knew for sure was that I didn't want to lose him.

"Good morning, beautiful!"

"Good morning, baby. Where do we go from here?"

"I don't know, Taylor, but I promise I will get this figured out."

"I trust you, Shawn. I have so many mixed emotions, but one thing I know is that I don't want to leave this hotel room again without you in my life. I want you, even if it means sharing you. Is that an option?"

"Well, I was leaning more toward me getting a divorce and being with you full time. It's hard right now because I am working full time and playing music, but I can't seem to get on my feet."

"Let me help you, Shawn!"

"No way! I don't want help from you that way. I just need that one big break. A chance to make it big."

"Shawn, I like who you are now. I can live a simple life. After I graduate from school, you can relax and play music! Forget about a big break. I will lose you if that happens."

"What? Taylor, you would never lose me for that reason. I need you. Please, give me some time. I will handle all of this. I will make you my priority! I will visit you as much as I can and I will call you every day. Give me a chance and I will give you the world someday."

"I will never leave you, Shawn. Let's do whatever it takes to make this happen. I am fine if you don't want to leave your family. Let's just take it slow and figure this all out. I would wait forever for you."

And so it began: the next chapter of my life. I sat in my windowsill staring out at the stars. The moon was full, and the bushes were full of fireflies.

Chapter Eleven

TAYLOR

I decided on my drive back home not to tell Kerrie or Donna about Shawn being married. For now, that would be just between us. I know that they would never approve of my decision to continue seeing him. Deep down inside, I didn't approve of my decision, but I also didn't have the strength to walk away from him. I was really okay with him staying married—for now, anyway. A better time could be when his kids were grown. I felt terrible for his family and I really believed that this was out of character for him. I hoped it was, anyway.

Heading to work, being in his arms was all that I could think about. The adorable dimples on his cheeks when he smiled. I loved the way he whispered in my ear when he was hugging me.

"Good evening, everyone."

"Hello, Donna!" I said with a huge smile on my face.

"Wow! Taylor, you look great! That must have been one awesome weekend."

"It was. I hated to come back."

I pulled up a barstool so that I could talk to Donna before my shift. "He was exactly as I remembered. When I walked into the club and made eye contact with him, I knew from that moment forward my life would never be the same. His touch, his kisses, everything was amazing. We spent the entire night together."

"Whoa!" Donna exclaimed. "Did you have sex with him?"

"Oh yes, multiple times. I don't think that either of us slept a wink that night."

"Oh Taylor, I am so happy for you, but I am also very jealous. Was there anything negative? Please don't tell me that you are moving to Oklahoma…I seriously would just die. Right here, drop dead."

I laughed till my face turned red. "We don't have plans just yet. I think it best we get to know each other better. He promised to come see me as much as he can and I will do the same. We have such a close bond that I don't think anything could keep us apart."

"Did you tell him that you work here?"

"No, we didn't cover that."

"Of course you didn't!"

"What does that mean? Do you think he would have an issue with me working here?"

"Well, it's a strip club and you dance on a pole for men for lots of money. It could go either way."

I was laughing, but I realized that she might have a good point. I guess I could cover that sometime down the road.

It was a Thursday night, and the club was hopping. I danced my ass off because it was the best night of the week. Businessmen would come in and drop copious amounts of money. On my breaks, I would take tequila shots. That always kept me going strong. It was liquid courage. I could work that pole better than any girl in the house most nights. I always kept my hair long. I found that the men seemed to be totally into dark skin and long, dark hair. I needed the money to get through school, so I did what I needed to do to make it happen. I usually walked away with a grand or more on a Thursday night. It was an upscale club, and touching was not allowed. It was often overlooked, however, for our more prominent clients. I was never ashamed of being a dancer. Donna did raise a good point, though. How would Shawn feel about this? Was I wrong to keep it from him?

The night went by fast and I was once again sitting at the bar drinking with Donna.

"Have you mentioned any of this to Kerrie?"

"I have not, but we need to all get together anyway, so let's get that planned!"

"Krispy Kreme?"

"You bet! I will text Kerrie right now and see if she is in."

An hour later, we were all three sitting on the ground on Westshore Boulevard, eating donuts and drinking milk. These girls were my ride or die sisters. Kerrie was excited to hear the news. I really expected a more negative response. Her biggest concern also was the fact that this could result in me relocating not only my life but also school. I worried about that too. School was everything to me. Being very bright, I never had to put a lot of effort into it. I was a straight-A student with nearly perfect attendance.

"Girls, I can't promise that I won't have to leave here, but I can promise that it won't be anytime soon. We want to get to know each other first—work out a few setbacks and issues first."

Kerrie quickly pulled "issues" out of the sentence.

"What issues?"

"You haven't mentioned issues to us yet."

"Well, not really issues. We just have things we need to work out first."

"What kind of things, Taylor? Get it out on the table. Isn't that why we are here?"

"Why? So the two of you can rip us apart?"

"No, so the two of us can talk some sense into you and guide you in a better direction if needed."

I was hesitant to say anything, but I had always been the weakest link of the three of us.

"Okay, please don't freak out or judge us. He is married…."

Kerrie immediately did exactly that. She freaked out.

"What? Taylor, you cannot break up this family. This is not who you are. Please tell me you will think about this more? Today it's a divorce so he can be with you. How long will it take for him to have another affair and leave you for another woman? Does he know anything about you? My guess is no. You were just convenient for him that night. Please promise me you will think about what you are doing. Does he have kids?"

I hesitated again. Kerrie and Donna both ganged up on me.

"You cannot do this! You cannot rip this family apart! Taylor, this will have a lasting effect on those children. You are both so selfish."

Donna really didn't say much. Kerrie would not give her a chance to speak. I was regretting this meeting already.

"Kerrie, we talked about all of this in depth! I told him I was okay with him staying married. I am totally fine being on the side for however long it takes. I'm in it for the long haul. Is it too much to ask that my two best friends withhold judgement and just support me through this? "I need you now more than ever. I really think I love him. I won't give up even if it means walking away from our friendship."

There was a long pause of silence. No one was saying a word.

"Taylor," Donna said with a grin, "we really should have bought more donuts!"

Chapter Twelve

TAYLOR

Months had passed since Shawn and I got together, and still very little had changed. I had very strong feelings for him. He often showed up at school without any warning and whisked me away for long weekend adventures. His music career did not seem to be progressing, and frankly, that was fine with me. I really didn't want anything to do with the fame, paparazzi, or fortune. He was writing songs all the time. I listened to them and I saw so many things that sounded familiar. I asked him if these songs were written about us. He blushed and pulled me over to where he kept his tablet of songs. He told me to look at the bottom right of the sheet. If it had my initials on it, then he wrote it about us. That was so sweet. I loved his music. He was an amazing artist.

"Taylor, I recently ran into some money problems, and I had to sell the rights to some of my songs, one of which I wrote about us before I found you. A brilliant upcoming artist sang it and soared to number one now two weeks in a row. I made a huge mistake selling it, but I really needed the money."

"It's okay, baby. It will happen for you again. I am sure of that!"

"I am here to take you away, baby. Where would you like to go?"

"You know what I would really love to do? I would love to just spend the weekend here at my place. Let's lie around and make love all weekend!"

"Wow! That sounds like a perfect weekend. When are you going to introduce me to some of your friends?"

I hesitated to answer, but I knew eventually I had to do it.

"Well, I'm just not ready for that yet."

"Why? Taylor, what is the issue with me meeting your friends?"

"Mainly because I had to tell them the truth. They both backed me into a corner and I had to tell them."

"You told them I was married?"

Sweat began to bead up on my forehead. I was a little angry and a little hurt.

"Why would you tell them that? You know I am working as hard as I can to get this fixed. Why would you do that to us? You know they are going to fill your head full of negativity."

"No, Shawn, they won't. These girls are like sisters to me. I admit they were negative at first, but we worked it all out. They understand we just need time."

"Then why can't I meet them?"

"Well, I guess we can get it arranged. Let's not do it this weekend, though. We can do it on your next trip."

Slowly I walked toward him, taking my clothes off piece by piece. He sat on the bed watching but not saying a word. I got close enough to him that he pulled me toward him and started kissing me. As he was kissing my neck, I slowly unbuttoned his shirt.

I could smell his cologne, and the scent was driving me crazy. I made it down to the button on his jeans. He stood up to help me get them off and slowly he laid me down on the bed. Still kissing me all over, he gently laid his body on mine and made love to me. Tonight was different. He was so passionate as he was gently thrusting inside me. Usually he preferred me on top, as he was quite a bit larger than me. He always had great endurance in bed and timing was never a problem.

I loved how he whispered in my ear, some of which I couldn't understand because I was too deep in the moment, but I totally loved it. We were perfect together.

We woke up three hours later, not realizing that we both fell asleep.

"Are you hungry, baby? I can fix us something here, or we can go out."

"Let's just eat here tonight, babe. Anything is fine. Do you have any tequila?"

"Of course I do! Let's have a drink first."

Well into several shots of tequila later, the doorbell rang. My heart stopped. I knew who it was. It was Donna and Kerrie. It had to be. No one else would ever visit me at this time of night.

"Are you going to answer the door?"

"Oh God, it's probably Donna and Kerrie. Can you hide until I get rid of them?"

"Absolutely not!" He walked toward the door and opened it. The greeting was silent and tense. He finally broke the ice by saying the first words.

"Hello, I'm Shawn. I have heard so much about the both of you, and I am glad to finally meet you."

Donna extended her hand and offered him a shake. Kerrie, however, did not. She totally refused to acknowledge him. The entire evening was tense and stressful. We exchanged some small talk and then the two of them were on their way.

"Wow!" Shawn exclaimed in a sarcastic tone. "I can't say I'm glad that happened."

I laughed hysterically to lighten the mood. "I tried to warn you! Donna is warming up, but Kerrie will definitely take a while."

"I feel so rejected by your friends. Is it really that big of a deal that I am married?"

"You mean married with kids?" I had to throw that in with a chuckle. "Let's have another drink. Forget about those two. They will find a way to get over it. If not, then maybe I need new friends!"

We continued to drink until the wee hours of the morning. I loved being with him. The thought often crossed my mind of where in the world his wife thought he was. Was she suspicious at all that he might be having an affair? I thought about her often and felt terrible about it all. Truthfully, if he was not with me, he would likely find someone else. I didn't think my leaving would save his marriage. He was obviously not happy. When we were together on these long weekends, I never wanted to fall asleep. The time always passed so quickly.

"Do you want to go for a walk?"

"I would love to, baby."

"I want to take you to a special place that my girls and I frequent to do our most profound thinking. It's a beautiful place where meetings are held and decisions are made. We have laughed there and we have cried there. It's on the bay downtown."

"I have to ask you, Taylor, have I been discussed there?"

I turned around and headed toward the door and exclaimed, "You betcha!"

Chapter Thirteen

SHAWN

⸻⟡⸻

*I*just had the most amazing weekend with Taylor. Every moment we spent together, I fell more and more in love with her. The last few months had been hell for me. The struggle inside my head and heart was becoming unbearable. I didn't know how to leave Nicole. We had kids together and our marriage wasn't terrible. She had to be getting a little suspicious. I spent all of my free time traveling to see Taylor. I couldn't remember the last time I spent a free weekend with Nicole and the kids.

I pulled into the driveway a little after midnight. I reached into the back of the truck and pulled out my guitar and a piece of luggage. My heart was beating fast and my hands were sweaty. I was always nervous when I came home after being with Taylor. The lights were off and everyone appeared to be asleep. I closed the door behind me with a little relief. I dropped my luggage to the floor and started walking toward the kitchen to get a beer. I heard a voice and it startled me. It was Nicole. She was sitting on the counter in the kitchen, waiting for me.

"How was your weekend?" Nicole asked in a soft but strange voice.

"It was okay. We played at a couple of bars in Tennessee. I'm really tired and seriously dreading going to work tomorrow."

"That's funny, Shawn. I saw John at the grocery store Saturday night. He said that you guys canceled your gigs this weekend. Were you playing music with someone else?"

I didn't answer. I grabbed a beer from the fridge and just walked away. I was not sure if I should just put it all out there and move forward with my plan or stay silent and see what happened.

"I found this manila envelope in our closet Saturday morning. Can you tell me what this is all about? You have been so distant lately. I can't help but believe that this may have something to do with it."

"Can I see the envelope?"

She handed me the envelope and I knew deep down inside there was no getting around it. I needed to tell her the truth. She deserved to know. I couldn't open it. I just held it in my hand and hung my head in shame. I sat down on a bar stool and ran my hands through my hair, as I often did when I got stressed or backed into a corner. We sat in silence for several minutes. You could have heard a pin drop a mile away. She waited patiently for me to answer.

"Her name is Taylor."

That's all I could get out. I started to get very upset and nervous. I was fighting back tears as I could see the hurt all over her face.

"Are you going to say something, Nicole?"

"I already know all about her. I knew her name before you did. I am confused and hurt. I just don't know what I did so wrong to make you want to step out on your family. Our kids. How will we explain this to our kids?

"Nicole, I never ever meant to hurt you or the kids. I don't know what happened to me. I was never looking to step out. It just happened. How did you find out? Was it John?"

"No! It was not John. I knew where you stayed that first night in the motel. I waited outside all night for you. I saw her leave the same room that you left the next morning. I did not want to approach her, but I did go to the front desk and the room was registered in her name. She is very pretty. She looks like a younger version of me."

Tears were falling down Nicole's face at this point. I was not sure if I should approach her or just stay seated and give her space. She was holding the countertop with both hands as if she felt like she was going to faint or something. My heart was so broken, yet I felt a sense of relief—relief that I no longer had to lie. I hated to lie. I have always been a man of my word, yet somehow overnight I had to lie almost every day.

"I am sorry, Nicole, for making you feel this way. I never meant to hurt you. My life just got out of control somehow. I feel like I work all the time, yet I never get anywhere. I was not looking for her or an affair at all. It just happened."

"Does she know that you are married?"

"Well, she does now. She didn't know in the beginning. She is a really good person. If she knew I was married, she would have never started or continued seeing me. Please, blame me. I am the bad guy here. Don't blame yourself or her. Where do we go from here?"

"Well, it depends. Are you willing to stop seeing her? I can forgive you, Shawn. I know you. This is not who you are. It's totally out of character for you. We all have had weak moments. Are you willing to promise to never see her again?"

I paused for what felt like eternity. I hung my head in shame once again and lifted briefly to say the words that no wife ever wants to hear.

"I can't say that I am willing to do that, Nicole. I love you so much, but…I also love her. If I have to make a choice right now, then I will have to say goodbye to you. I will continue to see and support you and the kids."

"Shawn, please don't leave. I will give you some time to figure this all out, but please don't leave me. I am sure this is just a fling for the two of you. I want to be here for you when it all ends. That's how much I love you. Is she married?"

"No, she is not."

We stood in the kitchen for hours talking about how we would handle this. I felt like such a jerk. Deep inside, I loved the idea of her not wanting to leave me. The thought also crossed my mind that Taylor also mentioned that she did not want me to get a divorce. Was it possible that I could keep them both in my life? As of right now, that seemed like the option that was on the table.

"Okay, Nicole, I think we should try to work through this. Are you agreeing that I can still see and speak to Taylor?"

"Yes, I will agree to that. I don't want anyone but us to know about this. I would rather live knowing about her than live without you."

Chapter Fourteen

SHAWN

The morning came early, and I was heading out the door to pick John up for work. I dreaded seeing Nicole. As I walked in the kitchen to pick up my lunch and say goodbye, Nicole greeted me with a smile and a kiss.

"Good morning, sweetheart. I hope you have a wonderful day at work. I love you so much. Please don't forget that."

She handed me my lunch and I headed for the door. I was a little confused and I really felt like a jerk, but I guess it was better than being angry.

John and I arrived at work right on time. It was gonna be another hot day. We were proud to work in the oil field. The work was hard and the hours were long, but if you had a job in oil you were somebody. Lunch time rolled around fast. I was so hot and sweaty but eager to get something to eat and drink.

"What's up, John?"

"Wow, you are in a good mood today! How was your weekend? Mine was great. I just sat at home and watched football all day. Did you go out of town with Nicole and the kids?"

"No, I went to Florida for the weekend."

"Oh," John said after a long pause. "How was that? Have you been making that trip often?"

"I have. John, I have been seeing her for several months now. Thank you again for getting the information for me."

John was silent. I could tell that he wanted no credit for getting Taylor and me together.

"Are we going out tonight after work?"

"Yes! Let's do! I want to tell you more about this past weekend."

I could tell John really wasn't sure he wanted to hear more, but I knew he wanted to drink. It was our nightly routine. We headed back to work. It was a hot-ass day and I couldn't wait for it to end.

We bolted out the door right at clock-out time, ready to hit the cool bar for a few cold beers. We sat at our usual table far in the corner away from most of the people.

"So, tell me about her."

"Well, she is amazing, fun, and so beautiful. We have spent several long weekends together. I can't find a single flaw. She loves my music, and we sing together all the time."

"Where does she work? I mean, what kind of work does she do?"

"You know, we have not discussed that yet. She goes to school full time. I know that she works at night, but I don't know where. I will ask her the next time we talk. I really cannot believe the topic hasn't come up."

"I was just curious, man."

"We have so much in common. She loves the outdoors as much as I do. I met a couple of her friends. I can't say the I enjoyed that. One of them would not even acknowledge my existence. The other one was just okay. She clearly had a problem with me, but she was nicer than the other one. It was not a pleasant exchange at all. I wonder how or if they will influence Taylor?"

"You really seem to like this girl, Shawn."

"I do. I cannot imagine my l life without her."

"Is Nicole getting suspicious at all? I saw her in the grocery store the other night. She seemed surprised that I was in town. We didn't talk much. I was a little nervous to say anything."

"John, she knows."

"What? How did she find out?"

"Apparently she has known since the first night I spent with Taylor. She saw her leave the same room that I left the next morning. Taylor was registered in the room and Nicole had a friend that worked at the motel get her the information. She just told me last night. I feel terrible, man, but I also feel relieved. Lying all the time was getting to me. I hate that I hurt her, but I am glad it's out."

"How did she handle it? I can't imagine how you both are getting through this right now."

"Surprisingly, we seem to be okay."

"What?" How can she be okay with your having an affair?"

"Well, she is not okay with the affair, but she said she also doesn't want a divorce. She thinks this will be just a short-lived thing and then our marriage will remain intact."

"Why would she be okay with this? You have never had an affair before, so why does she think this one would be short lived? I can tell you are in love with this other woman. I don't see you leaving her. How does Taylor feel about Nicole knowing?"

"I haven't told her yet."

"Wow. Do you think this will change things for her?"

"I'm not sure. She has also expressed concern about me getting a divorce."

"So let me get this straight—both of these women want you and both of them are okay with you staying with both of them?"

"Yep," I said with a huge grin on my face.

"Man, some people really do have it all. I can't find one good woman for myself. You now have two. Makes me wonder what the hell I'm doing wrong."

We shared a good laugh and left the bar. I dropped John off as usual and headed home. Nicole greeted me at the door. She gave me a hug and we headed off to bed. No questions and no drama.

Chapter Fifteen
TWO YEARS LATER

$\mathcal{T}$ime seemed to be flying by so fast. My marriage still seemed to be doing okay. Taylor and I were still in love, and it had been nearly two years now. I had three appointments this week with various producers in Nashville. I just felt in my bones that this was going to be my big break. Nicole was so excited for me. She had always been supportive of my dreams.

We were packing up, getting ready to head to Nashville. It was supposed to be my weekend with Taylor. I told her I had some family stuff that I needed to take care of. She had always been understanding when it came to my family. I was truly thankful for that.

Nicole and I loaded the truck and off we went. I was a little surprised that she chose to join me.

"Shawn, how does Taylor feel about you going to Nashville?"

"I haven't told her. She has made it clear to me that she wants nothing to do with this."

"With what?"

"Well, with me finally getting my big break—a recording contract."

"Oh wow! Are you a little nervous about how she will react when she finds out that you did all of this behind her back? I think you were wrong not to tell her. She deserves to know, and she will warm up to the idea eventually. What is her issue with it?"

"She is worried that fame and fortune will also bring an open-book life for us. Meaning, the world would soon come to find out about the relationship that I have with the two of you. She thinks the pressure will cause us to break apart and someone would lose. I know it's hard to believe, Nicole, but she really loves you and respects our time together. Any other woman would have forced me to make a decision. Taylor has always loved me unconditionally, even if that meant sharing me with you. She knows that at least in the beginning, I would have left you for her. She never wanted that to happen. She never wanted the girls to grow up without their dad."

"Shawn, I am so thankful for her. I know it seems weird, but in a way I think she has helped us keep our marriage together. You obviously were not happy at home and any other woman would have convinced you to leave me. I hope to meet her someday. When you go away on the weekends to meet her, it doesn't bother me like it used to. I feel a sense of relief knowing that I know who you are with. Having her in a weird way makes us better. I don't want to be critical, but I really wish you would reconsider telling her. She needs to be involved in this decision too."

"You really think so?"

"I really do. Now let's go in there and get you a record deal."

As we approached the door, anxiety started to set in. My mouth was dry and I was sweating in all the wrong places. Nicole really started to make me think about how I handled things with Taylor. I really wanted this contract, but I didn't want to lose her in the process.

I brought in a notebook with hundreds of songs that I had written. I was also equipped with a CD of a few of my favorites that I performed with the band. My guitar was thrown over my shoulder and I was ready to roll.

All of the interviews went well. They listened to my songs and also had me sing a few of them using only my guitar.

I had a good feeling leaving Nashville later that night. We got home well after midnight. I debated whether to call Taylor but decided there was no point in upsetting her if no one was really going to sign me.

At 6:00 the next morning my phone rang. It was Sunrise Records, and they made me an offer. I was so excited. I ran into the bedroom and woke up Nicole. "We got it!" I yelled at the top of my lungs. "I finally did it!" Tears rolled down my face as I held Nicole tightly in my arms. The phone rang again, and another offer was on the table. Wow! I now had two offers and a huge decision to make. I called in to work as I knew today was needed to get my head straight and make decisions about the rest of my life. I sat in my office for hours and finally decided to go with Sunrise Records. I never thought this day would come.

Nicole brought me in some lunch. A smile was planted across her beautiful face. She was genuinely happy, for this was going to provide a whole new life for us. We never had it easy. Life seemed to always deal us a bad hand.

"Shawn, I am so proud of you, but I am not surprised. You work so hard and so many hours; I knew that someday this would pay off. Have you thought any more about talking to Taylor about this?"

I pushed back my chair so we could talk. "I know I need to. I just fear it will be the end of us if I do. She has made her feelings very clear and there is no gray area."

I put my elbows on my knees and ran my hands through my hair. I know I had no other choice; I needed to include her in this process. Nicole approached me and put her arms around me.

"Shawn, I know if you handle this right and if she really loves you, she will allow you to follow your dreams. I know it will be hard at first, but isn't anything that is worth fighting for hard? I have the same worry that she has. I am terrified that the rest of the world will invade our privacy and expose our complicated situation. We will just remain careful and pray that we can lead a somewhat normal life with our children—Taylor included. I see how happy she makes you. I love you and if she makes you happy then she is worth fighting for....Now go call her!"

Chapter Sixteen

SHAWN CALLS TAYLOR

"Good morning, beautiful! How was your weekend?"

"Good morning, Shawn. You are up bright and early. My weekend was great. Since you did not come, I decided to put in a few extra hours at work. I'm a little tired but the extra money was totally worth it. School is getting expensive, so this weekend helped a lot."

"You know, all these years we have been together, I have never asked you about your work. All I really know is that you work at night. What exactly do you do?"

I skirted away to avoid answering the question. "It's not glamorous, but it pays the bills. Let's talk about you. How was your weekend with your family? Did you guys go out of town?"

"We did, actually. We went to Nashville."

"Oh, well, that's not the family outing I was expecting to hear about."

I giggled under my breath. "I really miss you, Shawn. I sure wish we lived closer together. I've been thinking about looking at schools near you to transfer to. What is your feeling on that? The upside would be I could see you more and you wouldn't have to travel so much. My biggest worry would be keeping our lives secret while living so close together. Here, no one really knows you so there are few risks. In

Oklahoma I feel like everyone would know some Joe that knows you. Do you think it would make Nicole uncomfortable if I moved closer?"

"Taylor, I think it would be great if you moved closer! Nicole still wants us to be discreet, but I think that she would be relieved that I would not have to travel so much. I say it's a win-win for everyone. There is something I need to tell you first, though. This trip to Nashville was not for pleasure. It was for business."

"What do you mean? Are you moving to Nashville?"

"I really don't know yet, Taylor. Please keep an open mind when I tell you this. I need you to really put thought into what you say before saying it. I love you so much. You have changed the fabric of who I am inside. I don't want to do anything to lose you."

"Come on, Shawn, what the hell is it?"

"I got a record deal. A good one. This is the break I needed and deserved. I have worked so hard."

Silence, total silence on the other end of the phone.

"Are you still there, Taylor? Please say something."

"I don't know what to say. My heart is crushed and shattered in a million pieces right now. I want so badly to be happy for you, but I know what this will cost. I have invested years in this relationship. I am not sure exactly what I was expecting. You are married with a family. Did I really think this would be my fairytale ending? I can't hold back the tears or my words. I am hurt beyond measure that you didn't prepare me for this. Did you think it was okay just to drop this bomb and I would be happy?"

"No, Taylor. This can still have a fairytale ending. Move, let's start a new chapter. It won't be ideal and it won't be a typical relationship, but we will have each other. Nicole has been so accepting of us. She wanted me to include you in this, but I knew how you would respond. I didn't want to tell you until I knew for sure that I would get signed. What is your biggest fear?"

"Once you sign, Shawn, the media will put our lives on the front page. I can't let both of our families bear the burden of our shame. I have to walk away. Not because I want to but because there are two little girls that need me to."

"Taylor, please don't do this. Help me build my dream. I can't do it without you. I won't."

"You have to, Shawn. This can be your fairytale ending, but it won't be mine."

I gently hung up the phone. Tears were flowing down my face as I sat in the windowsill staring out at the day. I was not sure if I was making the right decision, but I knew it was the best decision. I felt so lost and empty. I could not imagine my life without him in it.

I dialed up Donna, crying so hard I could barely speak. She knew it was donut time on Westshore. The three of us ended up there until two in the morning. I didn't know what I would do without these girls or glazed donuts.

Chapter Seventeen

SHAWN'S SUCCESSFUL BEGINNING

The very first album that I recorded hit number one on the charts three weeks in a row. The record went platinum almost overnight. My dreams were coming true, yet my heart was broken and my soul was empty.

Nicole came in my office later that evening with a cold beer and a sandwich.

"I am so proud of you, baby. I can see that you are in a different place right now. What is wrong? Is it Taylor?"

"Yes, it is. She won't even answer my calls anymore. I feel so broken and I cannot seem to find happiness at the cost of losing her."

"Don't sit around and pout! For God's sake, go! Go after her and show her this dream is worth fighting for! I can't bear to see you like this. The money will start rolling in soon. Take a trip with her. Bring her here. We can get through this together. If you lose her, then I also lose you. It is obvious that you love her. She seems to be an amazing woman. I know she misses you, too. She is just lost and confused right now. Show her this life is real and it's waiting for her to embrace it. If you don't go after her, I will!"

Hours later I boarded a plane for Florida. Nicole was right. I had to fight for her.

It was Friday night and I knew she would be working. If only I knew where that was. As I was sitting in the parking lot of the complex where she lived, a security guard approached me. He was an older man and a little crotchety.

"I'm waiting for Taylor. Do you know where she works?"

"Yes, Taylor. She is a sweet kid. She works at the Doll Haus downtown."

"The Doll Haus? Are you sure?"

"Yep, very sure. She has worked there three or four years now. Big money in it, I suspect."

"Thanks, brother. I will see if I can go surprise her."

My drive to the Doll Haus was tense. I could only hope she was a waitress there. I walked into the club. My heart was beating fast and my anger level was exploding. I looked at the stage and saw her. Taylor was a dancer. I waited at the bar, trying to calm myself down. She came off stage but had not noticed me yet. I walked over toward her as she was collecting money and about to give a lap dance. I grabbed her and pushed her to the floor. Picking her up, I proceeded to drag her out of the club and over to the car. I opened the door and shoved her in, hitting her head against the window of the car. I was unable to control my anger, and I ended up hurting her. I never meant to lose my temper that way, but seeing her dance half naked for money sent me to a place that I had never been before. I have never in my life hit a woman. Tonight not only did I do just that, but I broke the trust of a woman that I loved more than anything in the world. I felt terrible. Taylor had such a forgiving, understanding heart. That was what made her so special.

Her face began to swell, and she could barely move her neck. It became painfully obvious that I needed to take her to the hospital. During triage, Taylor told them that she was attacked in the parking lot of the night club. She lied to protect me.

A few quick X-rays were taken and the doctor came in to see us.

"Taylor," the doctor said in a surprised voice. "You, my friend, have a couple of fractures in you collar bone. These are going to take a while to heal. You also stated before the X-rays were taken that there was no chance that you could be pregnant."

"Yes, that's right."

"Well, the test just came back and you are pregnant."

"What? No, no, no. That can't be right. I cannot be pregnant."

Oh my God. All I could do was burst into tears. I just couldn't do this. My pain level right now was off the charts, yet I felt completely numb from head to toe.

"It's going to be okay, Taylor. Please calm down. We can get through this. We have gone through much worse."

I was torn between so may emotions. I knew Taylor would be okay, but I was not okay with the thought of her raising this baby without me.

TAYLOR:

"Shawn," I said in an emotional voice, my hands covering my face, catching every tear that fell. "How could this be happening? I can't do this by myself." I felt like every breath was being sucked out of me. I knew deep down that I had to do this by myself. I could not let this break up his family. I would be okay.

"Please, just go back home. Don't tell anyone. You are going to be big and famous soon. Don't let this scandal define the amazing artist that you are going to be."

"Taylor, I am nothing without you. I don't want to live without you. Let's pack you up and move to Oklahoma. We can keep this private. I don't care what we have to do, but you will not do this alone."

"How do you think we can hide this? Oh my God! What is Nicole going to think?"

"I won't leave unless you come with me. Taylor, forget about everything. Forget about school. Let's focus on our baby."

"Please, Shawn, I just need some time to think about it."

A sonographer came into the room and got me ready for an ultrasound. I was so nervous inside.

"We are just going to measure the baby and see how far along you are. Do a quick check and make sure everything is okay. Do you want to know the gender of the baby if we can see?"

Shawn eagerly spoke up. "Yes, if you can tell, we would like to know."

Shawn grabbed my hand and squeezed it.

"It's a boy!" she said in an excited tone.

Shawn put his face down on my hand and began to cry. He said, "I have wanted a boy for so long. He will be my legacy. It's a boy, Taylor! You are giving me a boy!"

My mind was in fifty different places. I knew that Shawn would never let me have this baby without him now that he knew it was a boy.

"Taylor, come back to Oklahoma with me, please. I will leave Nicole if that is what you want me to do."

"No! Absolutely not! You cannot leave her now. This will be a PR disaster! Please give me some space and time to think about all of this! In the meantime, please don't tell anyone except Nicole. I want this to remain private until I make my decision."

"Okay, but if you choose not to come back with me, then I want you to have this baby and give it to me."

"What? What are you saying?"

"I'm saying you will not take my son away. Nicole and I will raise him together as our own."

"How will I explain this to my friends and family?"

"You won't have to. We won't tell anyone. You will move to

Oklahoma where I will arrange your care and private delivery. No one will know, and if you choose to walk away, you can freely go, but my son stays with me. I will get a lawyer if I need to. By this time next week, I will be bigger than life, and trust me, you won't win this battle!"

My heart was truly broken now. I didn't think I would ever recover. I loved Shawn so much, and I never imagined him doing this to me. He finally left me alone in the hospital room where I stayed until the next morning. I prayed through the night. I came to the realization that he was right. He was bigger than me and he deserved his son. This decision would be hard to make, but I had to do what was best for my baby and his other family. If I asked him to leave Nicole, then two other children would lose their father. For me, that was not an option. I had to move to Oklahoma for the next seven months. My friends and family really wouldn't question it, because it was not unusual for me to go dark for months at a time. I knew I was in for a long, rough ride…alone.

Chapter Eighteen

PREPARING OKLAHOMA

───────•{───}•───────

I called Nicole that night after I left the hospital. I was still in a state of shock from everything that happened. Finding out Taylor was a stripper, me beating her up, and finding out she was pregnant. It was a horrible night to remember. I felt so guilty that I hit her. I felt even worse when I found out that she was pregnant. Could things get any worse?

"Nicole, we need to talk. I really made some mistakes tonight. I will tell you everything when I get back home."

"Okay. Shawn, are you drinking?"

"No. I have not had a drop, but my nerves have had all that I can take."

"What's wrong?"

"Taylor is pregnant."

Silence echoed through the other end of the phone. Nicole started to cry.

"Please, Nicole. Please don't cry. I cannot take much more. I lost my temper tonight. I hit Taylor and broke her collar bone."

"What? How did this happen?"

"I was shoving her into the car and it just happened. I snapped! I couldn't control it."

"Shawn, this is not who you are. You have never raised your hand to me. What in the hell happened?"

"I will tell you more later. Nicole, it's a boy. I told Taylor we would fight her and take him away or she could have the baby privately and you and I would raise him was our own."

"Shawn, we cannot take her baby away. You are not thinking clearly right now. I know you really want a son, but as a mother I cannot imagine the pain Taylor would feel every day if she were forced to give up her baby. I love you and I will do this with you, but only if this is what Taylor wants. Can I talk to her?"

"She will be released from the hospital tomorrow, and hopefully we will head back to Oklahoma."

"Shawn, do you still love her?"

"Yes, I really do. I want us all to be a family, and maybe you can convince her of that. I will never forgive myself for my actions tonight."

"Shawn, she will forgive you. Get some sleep. I will get a place ready for her."

"I love you, Nicole. I will be forever grateful for you. You have put up with so much from me. First another woman, and now a child out of wedlock."

"Shawn, we are a family. There will be no his or her children. No step or half siblings. We are one family. The world and society will have to deal with it if we can't hide it. Our love will persevere. I will talk to Taylor. Mother to mother. Please allow her time to make this decision. It will affect her for the rest of her life. I will support this, but only if she agrees to it. I cannot, as a mother, support your forcing her to give up her baby."

NICOLE:

After we hung up the phone, I poured myself a glass of wine and went into the living room to think. I felt so emotionally absent. The thought of Shawn hitting this girl was so troubling to me. To make matters worse, she was pregnant. I felt like our life was spinning out of control and there was nothing I could do about it. I was eager but nervous to meet Taylor. I really wanted to meet her, just not under these circumstances—broken bones and pregnant . Could it be any worse? What in the world went so wrong there tonight? Shawn was such a kind and gentle guy. It had to be something big.

I cried for a short while and then realized that I needed to pull It together. Hopefully he would be returning home tomorrow with her and we could all together figure out a way to work out this whole mess. I would support any decision that she made. I wanted her to know that I really did care about her. Either way, this baby would be okay. We would provide a loving home that he would thrive in. Hopefully together.

Chapter Nineteen

TAYLOR ARRIVES IN OKLAHOMA

*I*t was a long trip to Oklahoma. Every inch of my body was in pain. Very few words were spoken during the whole flight. I could tell Shawn was struggling with the decisions that he had made. I just wanted to get there and get it all over with. I had a lot of anxiety about meeting Nicole under these circumstances. I felt like crap. How would this go, exactly?

"Hello, I'm Taylor, your husband's mistress of the last several years. Oh, and I'm pregnant with his baby."

Nausea riddled my entire system. I felt like I needed to throw up.

"Let's go grab a bite before we get to the house. Do you feel like eating something?"

"I do. I'm a little hungry, but I am also very sick to my stomach. I have a lot of anxiety about meeting Nicole."

"Taylor, you don't need to stress at all about meeting her."

"How do you think she will react to the news?"

"She knows already. I talked to her about it last night. This won't be easy for any of us, but we will get through it. She was a bit shocked and hurt, but she seems to be more concerned about you. She really wants you to be okay with everything."

"What do you mean by everything?"

"Well, she wants you to be okay giving up the baby."

"Has that decision already been made for me?" I couldn't hold back the tears any longer. "I am trying so hard, Shawn, to be okay with this. I don't want to give you my baby, but I also don't want the world to know about us. I fear this would sink the career that you have worked so hard for. Deep inside, I just want to disappear. I want to go where no one knows me and have my baby and do this by myself. In fact, if you had not been there when I found out, you would never have known. I would have broken up with you and disappeared. Disappearing and running away is what I'm known for. I run from life. I want to run from all of this, but I don't feel that I can."

"Would you really leave me, Taylor?"

"I would. This whole situation is so incredibly uncomfortable for me. I never wanted any of this. Our relationship was so perfect the way it was. I never had to feel committed to you. I could be in love and not need to be with you full time. You would likely never know about my dark past and family secrets. I just want things to be the way they were. Simple. No drama and no strings attached. Let's eat and get this all over with."

We pulled into the driveway and my heart began to race. Complete fear flooded my soul. I felt faint and severely nauseated. We grabbed our bags and approached the front door. Shawn put his bag down and turned to me. With his arms around me he whispered in my ear, "Everything will be okay, darling. I promise you. If you get uncomfortable and want to leave, then we will leave together. I don't want you to feel alone or abandoned. I love you more than life right now, and if this costs me my career, then so be it. I don't want to lose you. No matter what."

I could not fight back the tears, and a few tears led to complete sobbing. Uncontrollable sobbing. Nicole walked out and immediately put her arms around me. Shawn gently let my hand go and stepped to the side.

"Taylor, I am Nicole, and I am so glad to finally meet you. I am sorry it's under these circumstances, but I will take it. I know how hard this all must be for you. I want you to know before you walk into in our home that I am on your side. I want to do what is comfortable for you. I want to get to know you."

An immediate calm spread throughout my body. I knew everything was going to be okay. Nicole was just as Shawn had told me she would be. We walked into the house. It was a small, cozy home. I walked around and looked at every picture on the wall. I realized this was no ordinary family. They were a loving, very tight-knit family.

"You all look so happy," I said to Nicole as tears continued to fall.

"We are happy."

"It makes me feel terrible inside that I almost destroyed you all."

"Oh Taylor, you never came close to tearing us apart. Shawn and I have always been strong, but we struggle, like any other married couple. Really, you have played a huge part in keeping us together over the past few years. The two of us were always enough for him. He has had plenty of opportunity to step out, but we keep him happy enough, I think. I was upset at first. I realized quickly that if there was going to be another woman, I would want someone like you. He said you were the reason he never left me. I made the decision that it was easier knowing about you then living without him. It's complicated but we will figure this all out in time."

"You must be tired."

"I am."

"Thank you for being so kind to me. I am so confused right now."

"Let's just continue all of this tomorrow. I have fixed up a bedroom on the lower level that you will be very comfortable in. Shawn has already taken your bags down."

I was blown away by Nicole's kindness toward me. I didn't know what I planned to do, but I felt so much better so far. I had no other options right now but to keep this all quiet to protect us all. It would be a long seven months. I could not imagine giving up a child. I never meant for any of this to happen. I loved Shawn so much. This was so complicated. I wanted to pray for guidance in all of this. My body was physically tired and my heart was emotionally broken. For the first time in my life, I was totally without direction.

Chapter Twenty

PREPARING FOR THE BABY

*S*everal weeks had passed and I was getting more comfortable with my decision. Nicole could not have been kinder. Every day, our relationship was getting stronger. I had barely seen Shawn. His career had taken off and he was in Nashville most of the time. When he was not recording, he was vigorously writing new songs. I was so proud of him. I really hated myself for not wanting to be part of his dream. Nicole deserved it more than I did. She was the one who had to endure being alone and raising children while he chased his dream.

I finally made my decision. I was going to let Shawn and Nicole raise the baby as their own. I would have to accept that I could only watch him grow up from afar. It would be too painful for me to stick around here and try to be in his life. Shawn and I would continue our relationship but agreed it was best that our son never know the truth. That protected us all. Every day, I was getting stronger and more confident with my decision. Shawn and Nicole would be great parents. I had decided to tell the few friends that knew I was pregnant that I lost the baby. I felt terrible lying, but I felt in my heart that it was best for everyone involved. Every other day, another media outlet was snooping around. No one so far had questioned anything. Nicole hated being photographed and constantly bothered by people wanting a story. I couldn't say that I blamed her. That was the very reason I never wanted anything to do with any part of Shawn's success.

Nicole and I were going shopping today. Her mom was going to keep the girls so it would be just the two of us on a stress-free, much-needed day on the town. I could tell she was getting excited about the baby coming.

We arrived at this amazing tea house. It was a perfect day for a high tea. We sat in a tiny corner of the café so that we could have some privacy.

"So, Taylor, how have you been feeling? Tell me everything. I want to share these last few days with you. I want to feel what you are feeling. Does he move a lot?"

"He does!" I said with a giggle. "He moves and keeps me awake all night long. Last night he had the hiccups. It was the strangest feeling. He is moving right now. Do you want to feel him?"

"Yes! Yes! I do!"

He was moving like crazy. It was a beautiful yet emotional moment that we shared together. We both teared up a little.

"Taylor, I am so happy that you trust me with the most important decision that you will ever make in your life. Shawn and I will give him a good home. He loves you so much. I really wish that you would stay around here in Oklahoma. We will find a way to make it work."

"I really can't, Nicole. My family and friends would never forgive me if they found out I did this. You see how we already have to hide and dodge the media. It's just a matter of time before some idiot finds out and shares it with the world."

"I understand. I totally get it."

"Do you think you could talk to Shawn about something? I would be so grateful if you would name him after my grandfather. Preston was his name. I loved him so much, and I was very close to him. He passed away, but I would like his legacy to live on through my son. I may never have another child, so this may be my only chance to honor him by passing down his namesake. I haven't mentioned this to Shawn because I want the two of you to discuss it in private. I know this is a sensitive subject, especially since I'm giving him up, so I thought it best if the two of you could think about it and decide together. No pressure from me, and I do understand if the answer is no. I also understand if Shawn wants him to bear his name and be a junior."

"Oh, I think it would be wonderful to name him after your grandfather. I love the name Preston. I am sure Shawn would be good with it, but I will do as you wish and discuss it with him in private. Do you really think that you may not want more children? Children are so amazing. A mother's love is powerful. I think someday you will change your mind. What if you have a boy in the future and we have already taken the name?"

"I have thought about this for weeks now. It's what I want to do. I would be so thankful if you would name him Preston. I cannot imagine being with any other man other than Shawn, sexually or emotionally. He is everything to me. I have also accepted the fact that what we have now is all that we will ever have in the future. I can't see myself having another child and complicating things further."

My emotions were overwhelming me, and I started to cry.

If Shawn was still the Shawn I had met when I was seventeen, we could have more. No one in this world would have given a damn about odd circumstances. I just wanted him to be an average working Joe.

"I am sorry that I am crying. I just don't want you to be uncomfortable."

"Taylor, I wish I could change things too. Don't think for a second that I am not concerned about how this fame and money will change our life. I am terrified; I know women will throw themselves at him. Will we be enough then? I struggle with these questions every day. If you want another baby in the future, I would be okay with you having one with Shawn. He loves you so much, Taylor. He wants everyone to be happy. I want everyone to be happy."

"I just can't see it, Nicole. I think this is a one and done for me. I will have to live secretly through you. My stomach really feels so tight right now." I bent over in extreme pain. "I think the anxiety is getting to me."

"Are you having contractions?"

"I'm not sure. I hope not. I'm not ready for this yet. Ugh! Oh, I think we need to go."

The pain was so bad that I couldn't stand up straight.

"I think we should call Shawn. He is in Nashville and it could take him a while to get here."

"I think we should, too. Nicole, he can't be with me in the delivery room. Will you please come with me? I really need you there."

"Taylor, I wouldn't miss it for the world, and I am so thankful that you want me there."

My pain level was through the roof. I was fully dilated, and the doctor said it should be anytime. Nicole had been a wonderful coach. On the next contraction, the doctor asked that I push with all of my strength. I was exhausted, but I knew I needed to get the baby out.

Just as I pushed, Shawn busted through the door. The nurses tried to get him to leave, but he refused. He announced to everyone in the room and God that he was the father and he was not leaving.

I pushed one more time and baby Preston came into the world. His proud daddy held him as the doctor cut the cord. Shawn handed the baby to me and I cried uncontrollably. I really began to question my decision to give him up.

The nurses took him away to clean him up. Nicole left the room. I could tell she was an emotional mess. I was, too. We all were.

Once we were in a private room, I started to feel better. Shawn never left my side while I was in the hospital. Preston was a beautiful baby. He had a head full of light-brown hair. He slept through the night and barely cried during the day. He cried only when he needed to eat or be changed. I did not breast-feed him. I thought that would be too hard for everyone. Especially me. Nicole helped with all of the feedings. I really wanted the two of them to bond. It would make it easier for me when I left.

Once we got the baby home, my recovery began. I needed to feel better so that I could leave and heal emotionally.

"Taylor, please, won't you reconsider my offer to stay? Nicole and I really do want you here. I love you so much and I don't want a life without you."

"Shawn, your recording contract sealed the deal for us. If you had remained an average Joe, we could have pulled this off. No one would have cared. You're big now! A big country music man. We can't pull off this lifestyle. Our children will never have a normal life. Please, let me go. I need to start a new life. I can't live here and watch you raise our baby with another woman. I need to move on, for everyone's sake."

"Taylor, my new album went platinum. The money is about to start rolling in. Let's get you a house here in Oklahoma. Please consider it. I don't want you to go. I want you to be part of Preston's life."

I went over to lie down on the bed in a fetal position, crying for what felt like hours. I was painfully confused. I was torn between what I wanted to do and what I needed to do. I thought the best thing for everyone would be for me to go—build another life and watch Preston grow up in pictures. I knew Nicole would support my decision. I knew in my heart this would be best for Shawn's career. He had worked so hard and he deserved this. I would go back and finish school and continue our relationship as it had always been: part-time and private.

Chapter Twenty-One

LEAVING OKLAHOMA

Going back to Florida was the right decision. I changed my major in school and decided to go into nursing. My aspirations to be a doctor were now a thing of the past. Kerrie was engaged to be married, so I really didn't see much of her anymore. Donna and I got together almost every weekend. Thanks to Shawn, I was able to keep my apartment here. He had always been good to me both emotionally and financially.

I worked all the time. It was not very often that I got to see Shawn. He toured a large portion of the year, and when he was not touring, he was recording in Nashville. Our love had not faded in the least. There was a part of me that thought it might be time to move on and have a normal life with someone else. Every time I tried, it ended up being an epic fail. Shawn was totally against me dating. He was extremely possessive of me.

My phone rang as I was leaving for work, and it was Nicole. I answered and was excited to hear her voice.

"Hey, Taylor! I wanted to see how things were going for you. I miss you so much."

"I'm doing okay. Getting in a routine has helped me move forward. How is Preston?"

"Oh my, he is a pistol. He is getting so big. His hair is starting to curl on the sides like his dad's. I was wondering if you might want to fly up and spend some time with him? Now is a good time because he is so young that he likely won't remember meeting you. We are building a bigger house and have bought up a lot of land near us. I wanted you to hear it from me first that Shawn is planning to build you a house, too. What are your thoughts on that?"

"Like a house near you?"

"Yes. On the ranch, actually."

"Wow, I really don't know how I feel about that. Would he do it expecting me to live there full time?"

"Well, I kind of think that is the plan, but I told him that he needed to talk to you first."

"I think it's a bad idea, Nicole. Preston is getting older, and I think it will start to raise a lot of questions. What are your thoughts?"

"I feel the same way. I love you and I would love you to be here. I get so lonely. Shawn is never home. Our life is so much easier now that we have money, but I don't have anyone to share it with."

"I think I would love to come visit, but moving to Oklahoma full time is not an option for me. I am struggling emotionally about giving up Preston. I just don't think I could bear to see you all every day. It would be a constant reminder of the decision that I had to make."

"I understand, and that's why I wanted to give you a heads up before Shawn just dropped the bomb on you. He is planning to come home Friday night for a week. I think he also plans to go out to visit with you if you don't have plans to come here."

"Nicole, I really want to see Preston. Could I just come there?"

"Yes! We would love that!"

Early Friday morning, I arrived. Shawn was not expected to arrive until well after midnight. This was my first time seeing Preston since I left. Nicole sent me pictures and videos almost every day. He was so handsome. He was starting to walk and get into things. It was a little heartbreaking to think that he would never really know me. He would never know my family or how much I truly loved him. Still, I didn't question the decision I made. I loved Shawn too much to end our relationship fighting over what was best for our child.

After Preston went to bed, I finally had a chance to talk with Nicole. We poured wine and sat on the front porch. I missed living in the country. The air was crisp and full of the songs of crickets. Fireflies lit up all of the bushes. It was a peaceful place that reminded me of where I grew up.

"Nicole, I am lonely too. I want to talk to Shawn about me moving on with my life. I love you both so much, but this is all I will ever have, and I just don't think it's enough. I can't imagine finding a man like him, but maybe if I could get close, I would have a chance to find happiness."

"Wow, Taylor, I really did not see that coming. I want to be selfish and say that I think it's a bad idea, but I get where you are coming from. How do you think he will feel about this? Have you mentioned this before to him?"

"Oh no! I have not. He gets crazy if I stop to speak to another man in the grocery store. I don't think this will be well received at all. I think if I do move on, it will also reduce the chance of our relationship being exposed. It protects us all, especially Preston. I plan to discuss it with him while I am here."

"I support whatever decision that you make, Taylor. That being said, I would rather have you here. It won't be the first scandal in the industry."

We shared a laugh and opened our second bottle of wine.

Hours later, we saw headlights pulling into the driveway. It was Shawn. Nicole decided to scurry off to bed so that we could have a chance to talk. When he stepped out of the truck, my heart just melted. I ran to him and he picked me up with his strong arms and twirled me around. He was a large man, well over six feet tall. He towered over me, and he was very muscular.

"Shawn, I have missed you," I whispered.

He took a moment and a deep breath and whispered back in a soft voice, "I have missed you too, baby."

"Did you get a chance to spend time with Preston?"

"He is so amazing. Our son is so amazing."

Tears began to fall.

"I see a lot of you in him. The way he holds eye contact when you speak to him reminds me so much of you. There is always a sparkle in his eye, and he is such a happy baby. His hair is curly now. He is looking more and more like me every day. I wish you would consider moving here. If I could make it happen and give you my word that everything would be okay, would you come?"

"Shawn, I can't. We would be risking everything. I actually came here tonight to ask you if you would give your blessing for me to move on with my life. I am so lonely, and a piece of my heart is here. I need to feel normal again."

There was a long, stressful pause.

"Taylor, what are you saying? Are you leaving me? Leaving us? You really don't want your son to know who you are? I am lost without you. You know me better than I know myself. I have to agree with Nicole on this. I would rather share you than to let you go. I don't want to share you, either."

"Shawn, you know darn well you won't share me. I love you so much, but where do we go from here?"

"From here?" he said. "We are going downstairs to your bedroom. I am going to make love to you, and we are going to talk about this tomorrow."

After making love and talking well into the morning, we were awakened by Preston crying. I ran upstairs to hold him before he woke Nicole up. Shawn struggled to make a bottle correctly so that we could feed him. Finally, we got it all together and made him happy. Holding him awakened something maternal in me. I felt like maybe I should give this life a chance. Every one of us all wanted the same thing. We wanted to be happy together. I dared not mention to Shawn that I was going to think about it, because he would never let me back out of it if I changed my mind.

Nicole came down and I had breakfast made for everyone. Shawn was walking around with Preston. She leaned over toward me and asked if we had a chance to talk.

"Yes, we did. Nicole, I am having second thoughts."

"Taylor, please say you will stay. Just give it a try."

Not realizing that Shawn was listening, I told Nicole that I was really wanting to try. I also was thinking that I may want another baby. With him. Preston would have a full sibling and I would have a second chance to make the right decision.

"Oh God, Taylor, I am so excited to hear this news. What is your hesitation in telling Shawn?"

"My only hesitation now is the risk. The risk of negative media attention if this gets out. I just want to protect you and Shawn."

Tears were in his eyes as he walked around the corner from where he was listening.

"I am a big boy. Let me handle this. I am prepared to lose it all if that is what it takes to have it all with you. I love you both so much. I do want more children with you. Let's do this. Our relationship is on a firm foundation. I am not worried about any of it at all."

I grabbed Preston out of Shawn's arms. Emotionally, I was all over the place. I had to try. We would do our best to keep everything quiet, but we were also prepared to do what we had to do.

I flew back to Florida a few days later. I put in my notice at work and said goodbye with very little explanation to my friends and co-workers. Construction was underway on my new life in Oklahoma. I sat in my windowsill one last time to think. It was a full moon and a warm night. I was not sure how this would all turn out, but I was sure that I had to try.

The fireflies were active tonight. I wished upon a few stars and walked away from that windowsill for the last time.

For the first time in a long time, my heart felt at peace.

Chapter Twenty-Two

A NEW LIFE

$\diamond$

My new life was underway in Oklahoma. I accepted a job at a hospital in Oklahoma City, and I couldn't wait to share the news with Nicole. I really struggled with the decision of whether or not I wanted to get a job, but it quickly became clear to me that it would be the best thing. I needed to stay busy. I loved spending time with Preston, but the older he got, the harder it got. I still struggled with my decision every day. I just didn't think that it would get any easier. I was still living with Shawn and Nicole. My house was almost finished, and I couldn't have been more excited.

Nicole and I were making supper together. In the evenings we always spent time with each other, talking about our day and catching up.

"Nicole, I accepted a job today. I will be working in the maternity ward in Oklahoma City. I am so excited."

"Wow, Taylor that is wonderful news! I would love to go back to work someday. Shawn hasn't really been supportive of that decision in the past."

"Really? Why?"

"I really don't know. I guess because of the kids. Preston is getting ready to start preschool now. I would really love to start looking for something."

"Nicole, I will support you any way I can. I am so happy to help pull the load with Preston. I can also help by doing things around the house. Even after I move."

"Thank you so much! How in the world did you convince Shawn to let you get a job?"

"Well, I didn't ask him. It never crossed my mind that I needed to. I guess I need to do that."

"I think you should." I giggled under my breath because deep down I knew what Shawn's reaction would be.

Dinner was amazing as usual, and we headed to the porch for our evening vino talks.

"Taylor, I am so glad that you are here. How are you liking it so far?"

"Well, so far, so good. I'm excited for the house to be finished, but I'm going to be sad in a way when it is."

"Me too. Shawn is never home, and I will be so incredibly lonely without you."

"Do you socialize much with the other wives of the band?"

"No, not really. I don't have much in common with them at all. John is really the only one, and even he doesn't come around much. He is a great guy. I never really understood why he never remarried."

"Remarried? Was he married before?"

"Yes, he was. His wife left him very early in their marriage. Ran off with some rich dude. Joke is on her now. John is rolling in the dough, and he has no one to share it with. I doubt he will ever trust another woman again."

"Wow! I didn't know any of this. Years ago when I first met Shawn, I could tell that John just wanted to stay out of it. He made it clear to Shawn that stepping out on you was wrong. He never really warmed up to me. Even now."

"Oh, don't take it personally. It's his own circus. I think he is getting used to it now. Tell me more about your friends, Taylor. Shawn mentioned one in particular. Donna? I think that was her name."

"Yes, Donna is one of my closest friends right now. I met her in college and we immediately bonded. We also worked together. In a night club...."

"Oh Taylor, please tell me more." We both giggled.

"We need to open another bottle of wine if you want me to spill the beans on this."

We opened another bottle of wine and the facts started flowing.

"Donna and I were both dancers at the club. Our names were Sunshine and Rain."

"You really are an interesting person, Taylor. You are like an artichoke. I keep pulling back one interesting layer after another."

"When Shawn snapped that night when he came to visit me in Florida, it was that night that he discovered that I worked there. I had just collected money to give a lap dance when he grabbed me and threw me to the floor and dragged my ass out."

Nicole just stared at me, saying nothing.

"I am lost for words. That is just not the Shawn that I know. I always wondered what happened that night, but I was honestly afraid to ask. Nothing in this life is worth hitting or hurting someone that you love. I know he sucks with apologies, but did he ever really try to apologize for what happened that night?"

"No, and that's okay."

"No, it is not okay. It's not okay at all. You did nothing to deserve that."

"I have learned to let a lot of things go over the years. I kind of feel like I deserved a little punishment for the hell we put you through."

"What hell? I never felt like you put me through hell. Shawn was really very open when it came to you. He worked and played in bars every weekend. It was bound to happen sooner or later. I'm just glad he found someone like you. He never lied once I confronted him. He is such a good man, Taylor. I hope you realize that. He would take a bullet for either one of us. When he stepped out with you, I know that he had never done that before. No doubt in my mind. He is an honest man."

"I know he is. I cannot imagine my life without him. There was a part of me that wanted to move on and start a normal life, one where I didn't need to explain any of this, but I soon realized that this is all I really wanted. I can't imagine life without you. Getting back to Donna, I was thinking of inviting her to come visit. I really need to tell her about us. I don't want her to know about Preston. I don't want anyone to know."

"Did she know that you were pregnant?"

"Yes, she knew. I told her that I lost the baby. No one questions when you tell them that. Donna was my best friend. I miss her so much. She will love you. She will be very opinionated about our life-style, so brace yourself for that. She wanted me to end things with Shawn once she found out that he was married."

"I would really love to meet her. Once she sees how we make this all work, I think she will be a little more understanding."

"Nicole, have you ever told anyone about any of this?"

"I have not. Once I found out that you were pregnant, I went into hiding, avoiding everyone. I told most people on the phone that I was pregnant and on bed rest. No one was surprised or questioned anything when we brought Preston home. I really tried to think of everything.

"Taylor, I am not ashamed of any of this. I am only hiding this for you, because you asked me to. Shawn and I have talked about this a lot. Neither of us has any regrets. We are not ashamed of the choices we have made. If there comes a time that you want the truth to set you free, we are fully prepared to do just that. Until then, we will remain quiet and private. That's what we do as a family. We lift each other up and support one another."

"Nicole, I feel very fortunate to have you and Shawn in my life.

Somehow I feel like this is all meant to be." I'm going to call Donna tomorrow and see if I can get her to come up for a visit. She actually went to see Shawn in concert in Mississippi last month. She said she absolutely loved him. I wanted her to meet up with him after the show, but she refused. Eventually, she will warm up to him. She thinks eventually I will get tired and come home. I really want to bring her here and show her what life is really like for me."

"It's getting really late. I think we should call it a night. We are also out of wine."

We shared a laugh and with arms tucked around each other, we went into the house and retired to our bedrooms.

Chapter Twenty-Three

DONNA'S VISIT

Fall was in the air and the weather was rapidly changing. My house was almost finished, and I could start another chapter of my life. It had been weeks since we had seen Shawn. Thank God Nicole and I had each other. Preston was so rambunctious. I really enjoyed waking up to him every morning. He was the light of my life right now. I would miss him when I moved to my own house. I was thinking about asking Nicole if I could have some days with him—maybe weekends or a couple of days during the week. I would be thankful for any amount of time that I could get. That would also give Nicole a break. I think she would be totally fine with it, but I would save the question for a wine night.

Donna was coming in for a visit and would arrive tonight. I was so excited to see her and share my new life with her. I was going to get my hair and nails done before I picked her up from the airport. Donna had always been critical of my appearance, although she would never admit it.

"Nicole, I am going to pick up Donna after I get my hair and nails done. Would you like to join me?"

"Oh, I would love to go with you. Let me call around and see if I can get a sitter for Preston. We could also go out for drinks after, if you want."

"That sounds like a great plan. I could really use a night out!"

My phone rang just as I was heading downstairs to get dressed.

"Hey Shawn! It's so good to hear your voice! Nicole and I are heading out soon to pick up Donna from the airport. She is going to come and visit us for a week."

"That's great news, baby. I miss you so much. I was hoping to get home this week, but maybe I should wait until she leaves. I'm not exactly her favorite person right now."

"Oh, she's okay. I think it's good that she is coming here. It is easy to see how happy we all are."

"Do you plan to tell her everything? Are you going to tell her about Preston?"

"No, I don't think so. She thinks I lost the baby, so I think we should just leave it there for now. "Shawn, are you okay?"

"What do you mean?"

"Well, you sound like you're slurring a little bit when you talk."

"No, baby. I'm okay. I am just exhausted. I work all the time. If I'm not writing, I'm recording or doing interviews."

"Have you been drinking?"

"Hey, is Nicole around? Never mind, just have her call me later, if you don't mind. I just want to say hello. I love you all so much."

"Okay, baby, I will have her call you later."

I headed upstairs and Nicole and I left to pick up Donna. We dropped Preston off with Nicole's sister. On the way to the airport, I decided to ask to Nicole about sharing some days with Preston. She thought it was a great idea. It would give her a much-needed break. I really had that to look forward to after I moved.

"Nicole, Shawn called just as we were getting ready to leave. He asked me to have you call him later. Have you talked to him recently?"

"It's been about a week. Why? Is something wrong?"

"Well, he just sounded a little funny. His speech seemed a little slurred. I think he had been drinking, although he totally denied it."

"Taylor, I didn't want to tell you this, but I have noticed it too. For several months, actually. It seems to be getting worse."

"Do you think he has a drinking problem? I am really worried about this. I really had no idea. I have noticed a slight slurring in the past, but it never crossed my mind that he was drunk."

"Do you think this is an issue that we should be worried about? Has it been an issue in the past?"

"Yes, it has been an issue before. Sometimes Shawn just gets overwhelmed with life, and he always turns to the bottle. Let me talk to him tonight. Let's not assume the worst. He is surrounded by good people. I feel like if there was a problem, one of them would tell me."

We met Donna at the airport. Our hug was so emotional. I just began to cry uncontrollably. Part of it was my excitement to see her, but another part was my worry for Shawn.

"Donna, this is Nicole."

Donna extended her hand to her.

"I am Donna. Taylor and I go way, way back."

"I am Nicole, Shawn's wife."

"Oh!" Donna exclaimed. "Taylor failed to mention that I would be meeting you. Pardon my incredibly uncomfortable response right now."

"Oh, there is no need to be uncomfortable, Donna. Taylor and I will fill you in over drinks."

We climbed into the car and headed to a little local bar. It was our go-to watering hole near our house. After a few drinks, Donna really began to loosen up a bit.

"Nicole, you are really one of the sweetest people that I have ever met. Frankly, I thought Shawn was an asshole. I guess I should give him a second chance."

We all laughed. We needed that breakthrough.

"Taylor, you look like you are doing so good here. I am so glad that you found happiness. I do miss you terribly. There is no Sunshine after the Rain anymore."

I giggled, but I really deep down missed dancing in the club. It was such a high, and a lot more money than nursing.

We were all getting tired, so we headed home. I showed Donna to her room, and we all went to bed. Preston woke up earlier than usual. I rushed upstairs to grab him before Nicole woke up. He was such a sweet boy. He was ready to eat breakfast before the sun came up this morning. I fixed him some eggs and a biscuit, and he sat on the sofa and watched cartoons. He loved *Cars*. It was his favorite show. He was content to watch, so I went back downstairs to take a shower and get my make-up on.

Donna woke up and went upstairs while I was still in the shower. I could hear her opening drawers, so I went up to see if I could help her find something.

"I'm just looking for some tea. Do you have any?"

"Of course. Come over here, and I will show you my tea drawer. Donna, you have a weird look on your face. Is there something wrong?"

"Something wrong? Well, for starters, Taylor, I walked into the living room because I heard the TV. Who is the little boy in there?"

"His name is Preston."

"Okay, who is Preston? I have not heard you mention him."

"Donna, It's so complicated."

"I bet it is, Taylor! Do you realize how confusing this whole mess is for him?"

"No, he is a happy, healthy little boy. Spend time with him, and you will see that he is not the least bit confused. He is a great kid."

I was nervous about what Nicole might think or guess as she watched us together. My phone rang and I quickly rushed to pick it up. I knew it would be Shawn.

"Hey, baby, how are you doing?"

"I'm doing good, sweetheart. Did Donna arrive okay?"

"She did. We are having a great time so far. Nicole and Donna aren't exactly bonding, but we are all having fun. When are you coming home?"

"I was thinking I would come home tomorrow night. I'm so tired. I just need a few days to sleep in my own bed. I will stay out of you girls' way."

"Shawn, I can't wait to see you. You will not be in our way at all. I think it will be good for you to come while Donna is still here. I really want to talk to you anyway about some things that have been on my mind."

"Okay, kitten. I love you. I will see you sometime tomorrow night."

Donna and I stayed at the house and hung out by the pool all day. We needed a full day of girl talk to just catch up on all things important since the last time we talked to each other.

"So, Taylor, is your plan to just live here long term with Nicole and Shawn?"

"Nooooo, it is not. I am building a house down the road not far from here. It will be ready very soon, and then I will be moving out."

"Will you be taking your son with you?"

"What?" I exclaimed in a high-pitched, freaked-out voice. My heart felt like it was beating out of my chest.

"Will you take Preston with you?"

"Donna, I told you already, Nicole is Preston's mother."

"Taylor, please don't play me for a fool. You are so maternal with him. He looks just like you around the eyes. It would take a complete idiot not to realize that you are in fact his mother. And Preston, let me think, wasn't that your grandfather's name? Is that why you are here?"

"Donna, please. This is all so complicated."

"It's okay if you don't want to tell me the truth. You'd better be prepared, because no one in this world is going to buy this bullshit story. I am your best friend, and you still felt like you needed to lie to me? I just don't understand why. Why all of this weirdness and dys-function? What is the big deal with just being a single mom? Don't you know that someday he will find out about all of this? He will be crushed. Kids never get over this kind of stuff."

"I never really thought about it that way. He is loved by us all. We just all thought it would be best if Nicole and Shawn raised him and I just lived in the shadow. I love him so much. I want to watch him grow up as much as possible. Please, Donna, don't ever speak of this to any-one. We have to keep this private."

"You have my word, Taylor. I am just in a state of shock right now. I will never betray your trust. I just have one question. Did Shawn force you to give up your baby?"

"Yes, in the beginning he did, but I soon realized that it would be the best thing anyway."

"Are you sure you are okay with your decision? Is this something that you can live with the rest of your life? I don't know that I could. I really hate him. I really hate what he is doing to you and how he is changing you."

"Donna, please."

"No! Taylor, none of this is okay. What is it about this guy that keeps you hanging on? He is cruel and selfish. What man takes a child away from a woman?"

"Donna, I can't do this by myself. The entire world worships him right now. He threatened me to agree to it. I admit that after I did it, I regretted it, but I felt like it was too late to back out. Please try and understand. He is not a bad person. He is amazing, and I need him in my life. He has tried in so many ways to make this right. What do you expect him to do?"

"Did he pay you to give up your son? Are you doing all of this for money?"

"Really, Donna, he was broke as shit when I met him and for years after."

"No! Now, is he paying you now?"

"He has given me money, I admit that, but that is not why I stay."

"Really?"

"Yes! Really. He gave me a substantial amount and it's in an account. If I was doing this for the money, I could leave now with all of it. It's not about that. In fact, I have never used a dime of it. I don't want it. I want to be here with the family I love. I need one person in my life, Donna, who can love and support me through all of this. I have never needed you more."

"I'm sorry, Taylor. I can't be that person."

Chapter Twenty-Four

I sat outside later that night having a glass of wine with Nicole. My heart was so heavy, and I was really beginning to question whether or not I was doing the right thing. I was torn between what my heart wanted me to do and what I should do.

"You look like you have a lot on your mind tonight, Taylor. Is everything okay?"

"No, not really."

I set down my glass of wine to wipe the tears that were rolling down my face.

"I am not okay. I don't know that I will ever be okay again."

Nicole came over to me, putting her arm around my shoulders.

"Talk to me. I am here for you. Is this about Shawn?"

"No, although that is weighing on my mind too. It's Donna. She asked me today if Preston was my son."

"Wait, what? Why would she ask you something like that?"

I could barely speak. My whole body was shaking uncontrollably and Nicole was doing her best to calm me down. In the distance down the driveway, we saw headlights.

"Taylor, it's Shawn coming down the drive. We really need to calm you down a little bit. You know how crazy he gets when he sees either one of us upset. He will snap."

"I'm really trying. I can't stop whatever is happening right now."

"Okay, Taylor, what can I do to make this better? We can reverse all of this if you want. Preston is old enough to remember a little, but kids are resilient and he will be fine. I'm worried about you."

Shawn could tell something was wrong as he drove up. He jumped quickly out of the truck and ran over.

"What's going on?" He grabbed me up and embraced me in a hug, his large hands cupping my head and neck.

"What's wrong, baby? I'm here. Please, calm down."

The tears just kept coming, and my body continued to tremble.

"I'm never going to be okay. You both have done so much for me and I want to be comfortable with everything, but I just don't think that I can. Donna was here a week and already she is questioning me about Preston. How are we going to pull this off with the rest of the world if we can't even fool Donna? I don't even know what I want anymore. I just want to love you all out loud, but I know that I can't right now, and I am not sure that I will ever be able to."

Shawn sat down on the porch step just looking out into the night.

"Preston is getting older. We have to decide how this is going to work going forward."

"Taylor, I don't know how to handle this either. I know that I have left this tremendous burden for the two of you to bear . I can't stand the thought of losing you, and whatever you decide to do, I will support you in that, but Preston stays here in Oklahoma. I really want you to stay, and I am prepared for any backlash from the media and the world. I can handle it. My fan base is solid, and most of them will support us through this. We can do this together. Please don't leave me."

"Shawn, I am lost for words. I can't stand the *what-if* side of this. I don't want you to risk your future. Your future is Preston's future. I don't want it to be tainted with scandal. I think it best that I go. I will always love you both, and I hope we can continue our relationship, but I can't do this. I can't do this to our son."

Nicole got up and walked away. I could tell that she was crying.

"Shawn, I feel like I have hurt everyone. This outcome would have been so different had you not been there at the hospital that night when they told me that I was pregnant."

"What do you mean by that, Taylor? Are you telling me you would have hidden all of this from me? My only son?"

"Yes, I would have. We would have broken ties and both would have moved on by now. I would have been fine being a single mother. I'm in hell right now. You have have no idea how hard it is losing a child. Now I have to lose him all over again. It's killing me inside. I am prepared to move on. I will leave half of my heart here. I think it best that I watch him grow up from afar. It's for his own sake and future.

"He will be your legacy, Shawn. I will always be his mother, and nothing in his world will ever change that. I think I want to move back to Santa Barbara. I can get a job there and start a new life where no one knows me. I hope you will still want to be part of my life. I can't imagine losing everything right now."

"Taylor, I will always be part of your life. Nothing will ever change that. The house we built here will always be yours to come home to. Nicole is going to take this hard. I am just sick inside at the thought of losing you, too. I knew this would be hard for you, but I was hopeful. Can you promise me one thing? Promise me we will be together full time someday. Promise me that you will marry me. Please don't give up on us. We have to many years and memories invested here. I wish things were different. I wish we lived in a more forgiving world."

"I will make that promise to you, Shawn. I will be your wife someday. Maybe when you retire, we can try to build this life together again."

We embraced in a hug that night with a lot of big promises made. Only time would tell if they would be kept.

Chapter Twenty-Five

TAYLOR IN SANTA BARBARA

⌣—⌣

With very little planning, I left Oklahoma and half of my heart in the middle of the night. Deep inside, I knew that my life would never really be the same. I didn't think it was possible that I would ever find happiness, but I needed to try. I grew up on the East Coast and although I didn't think I could ever go back there, my soul needed to be near the ocean.

I lived and worked in Santa Barbara a few years ago and I really loved it and had really always wanted to go back. The weather was always perfect—warm and breezy, and the sun was always shining bright. I could spend every day of my life on the beach. The warm sand and the smell of salt water in the air had a grounding effect on me. I needed to heal emotionally, and this was where I needed to do it.

I rented a cozy beach house on the water. It was small, but plenty of room for me. The inside was painted with bright colors of turquoise and coral—not exactly the colors that I would choose, but it would have to do for now. There were lots of windows to open for a fresh breeze and salty air.

I watched the sunset over the water every night on the deck. Unlike my house in Florida, I didn't have a good sunrise view. I was okay with that. The sunrise only reminded me of Shawn. We used to watch the sunrise every morning that we were together. It was a symbol of a new day and another day closer to the life that we both wanted. The sunset for me now was going to be a symbol of closure in my life. I needed to close this chapter and move forward with a new one. I wanted to be the person that I used to be—happy and independent. I was tired and worn out with life. The hardest part to deal with was leaving Preston behind. He was growing up and would be an amazing young man someday. I wished I could be part of it. I wondered if he would ever know who I was? Likely not, because Shawn insisted on a closed adoption. The records were sealed, and chances were he would never even know he was adopted.

My focus these next few months was going to be therapy and healing. I started seeing a really good therapist who hopefully would offer some support and guidance so that I could be successful in moving on with my life. It wasn't that I wanted to forget about Shawn. I knew I would never be able to do that. I just thought that if I could start a new healthy relationship with someone else, that would be the best thing for all of us. I wanted to still talk to Shawn and Nicole and be a big part of their lives; I just needed it to be with different circumstances— a relationship that the rest of the world would accept. My therapist disagreed with me about this. She thoughts that I was running away from what I wanted in life just to please other people. I really didn't think that was it at all. I wanted to protect those that I loved the most. I wanted to protect my son. I didn't want him to have the burden of negativity if the rest of the world found out the truth.

Against the advice of my therapist, I started going out more. I always struggled to meet men, I think because subconsciously I just wanted to be with Shawn. I found it hard to open my heart up to anyone else.

It was early spring and a bit chilly outside. The air was crisp and a bit cold. I went to a little dive bar not far from where I lived. When I say dive bar, I don't mean trashy or dirty. It was just small and mostly catered to locals. I never knew anyone in there, but everyone else seemed to know each other. I went there a couple of nights a week. The bartender was a hoot. I'm pretty sure that he was gay, and he was always spot on with advice that he gave me. He always commented about my hair or the clothes that I was wearing. His name was Simon. He told me that a gentleman had been asking about me a few nights ago and wondered if I was single. I quickly responded with a great big yes and said I was eager to meet him. This was my goal! I wanted to meet someone and start a new life.

"He is sitting at the end of the bar. Go over and talk to him."

No way could I do that. I could never approach a random guy. Especially in a bar. He was gorgeous—dark hair, and he had the broad shoulders of a marine. I could not imagine why he would be interested in me. He got up off of the bar stool and was walking over toward me. I was extremely nervous, but I tried to convince myself not to act like a fool. He held out his hand as if he wanted to shake.

"Hello, I'm Bo. Bo Thomas. Your name is?"

"Taylor. My name is Taylor."

"Are you new around here? I have never seen you in here before."

"Well, I'm a little new. I recently moved back here from Oklahoma. I used to live here years ago, and I decided to come back."

"What's your story, Taylor?"

"There is no story, really. It's complicated. I'm complicated. What's your story, Bo Thomas? Are you from around here?"

"I am. I grew up here. I work for the Border Patrol and Homeland Security. I love California, and most of my family still lives here."

The bartender kept the drinks coming. Bo was really growing on me. He seemed like a great guy. We talked until the bar closed that morning. I think he could tell that I was very nervous to share much with him. I wanted a clean slate, a new foundation to build on. I can't lie. I was a little nervous about his line of work. I knew it was a thankless and scary job. I wasn't sure that I was ready or willing to hook up with a guy that I had to worry about every night. I needed to put some thought into that. Otherwise, I really really liked him.

"The bar is closing now, so I guess we need to leave. I have to admit, Taylor, I have really enjoyed meeting you tonight. Is there a chance you would want to see me again?"

"I would love that."

"Can I walk you out to your car?"

"I walked here. I live really close, but thanks anyway."

"I walked here too! Let's go, we can walk out together."

As weird fate would have it, he lived down the road from where I was living. We walked home together and shared a lot of laughs. Wow! This was exactly what I needed. I needed a good distraction, and I certainly thought that I found it tonight. It's amazing how much you can learn about somebody just by sharing a few hours together on a bar stool. He was the whole package—gorgeous and kind. He was full of energy and could also carry on an intelligent conversation. I couldn't say that about most men that I had dated in the past.

As our walk and our night came to a close, he turned toward me and asked my permission to kiss me. With excitement, I accepted his request. His lips touched mine and my whole body leaned in toward him. It was nice to feel that spark again. The taste on his lips was sweet. He placed his hand gently on the side of my face and finished up by kissing me seductively on my forehead. I wanted to invite him in, but I knew it was just too soon. He grabbed both of my hands and said good night. I watched him walk away. He left without my phone number or asking me out for a future date. I couldn't let him go.

"Hey, Bo Thomas, I would really like to see you again!"

"Ditto!" he said as he waved his hand in the air and continued to walk away.

That was it—and he walked away with the most adorable smile on his face.

Ditto? What was that code for? I giggled for a bit and went inside and got ready for bed. I didn't dream of Bo that night. After the fun night I shared with him, I still couldn't get Shawn off of my mind. He was like a disease to me.

Chapter Twenty-Six

The sun was barely up, and I had already run five miles and was on my second shot of espresso. I was giddy with excitement after meeting Bo last night. My cell phone rang and it was Simon, the bartender from the dive bar.

"Hello, beautiful lady!"

"Hello, Simon."

"You know why I am calling, so go ahead and fill me in."

"Oh goodness, Simon. He is so amazing. He was so much fun and a perfect gentleman at the end of the night."

"Ugh, I hate to hear that. I was really hoping that you got laid last night."

I laughed so hard that I almost dropped the phone. The doorbell rang and I peeked out of the kitchen window.

"It's Bo!"

"Oooh, goody! Please call me as soon as he leaves and fill a brother in."

I answered the door and acted surprised that it was him. He held out a bag of pastries and said good morning. I made us a pot of coffee and we sat on the deck and talked for hours. We talked about everything. I could tell that he really enjoyed talking about his family. He was especially close to his mother. His dad left his mom a few years ago, and I could tell that was an uncomfortable issue for him. He asked me if I had children. How was I supposed to answer that? I felt like I had to lie. After all, I really barely knew him. There was no point in sharing that whole story with him. So I lied. He also asked if I wanted children in the future. I also lied. Wow, this relationship thing was really starting out on the wrong foot. A big mountain of lies. I couldn't really tell him the truth—not now, anyway.

It was getting close to 3 p.m. and he said he needed to go and get ready for work. That's where the day went from lies to worse. I ask him what time he got off, and he said midnight. He also proceeded to tell me that he was working for Santa Barbara PD tonight. PD as in police department . Good grief. I could never be involved with a cop. I worried too much. I would never sleep again.

He embraced me in a goodbye kiss—the kind that leaves you weak in the knees. To close the kiss, he gently rolled his tongue across my lower lip. I just melted.

"Can I see you tonight?"

Without any hesitation at all, I said yes. I couldn't wait to see him again. Chills rolled up and down my spine as I walked him to the door.

I watched him walk up the road until he was out of sight. I couldn't wait to call Simon and tell him everything. I looked at the clock and realized that the bar was open, so I got dressed and headed down there to share my news with him. I really needed his advice, more than anything. I needed to know if I should feel this much guilt for moving on with my life. I had spent many nights down at the bar, and every night I would fill him in about my life and past that I was trying to leave behind in Oklahoma.

I walked into the bar, and Simon ran to the door and hugged me. He was clearly excited to see me.

"Fill me in, honey, and don't leave a single detail out."

"Well, long story short, he brought breakfast over and I am pretty sure tonight will be the night. Should I feel guilty about any of this? Because I do. All I can think about is Shawn. I don't want to, but I do. I want to be over him. I really do want to move on with my life."

"Taylor, my love," he said as he leaned in toward me. "The only way to get over Shawn is to get under another man. It works for me every time."

We shared a much-needed laugh.

"I know it feels strange right now, but you need to move forward with your life. Bo is a great guy. I have known him for years. He comes into this bar almost every night after work, and in all these years I have never seen him take to a woman the way he took to you. You really should give him a chance. He could be the one."

I knew that Simon was right. I needed to move on with my life, and Bo was a great place to start. Plus, I needed to get laid. I would be sleeping with him tonight if I had to tie him up and force him to do it.

I left the bar with a whole new perspective on things. I needed this. I was going to get dolled up super sexy and leave him no reason to wonder if I was ready to sleep with him.

At 1:15 a.m., my doorbell rang, and I answered it wearing a sheer black sexy nightgown. He walked in and never said a word. He picked me up and walked me over to the sofa. He lay down on top of me, kissing me while I struggled to unbutton his shirt. He was still wearing his uniform, which I found very sexy. He stood up and undressed slowly while I watched him. He slipped down beside the sofa and seductively removed my panties. We made love several times that night. It was amazing. He was way better than I expected him to be. I wasn't sure why I expected less.

He spent the night with me and I woke up with no regrets, which I thought was a very good sign. Bo made it very clear that he wanted to continue seeing me. He also made it very clear that this whole situation was totally out of character for him. He didn't want me to think that picking up girls in a bar and sleeping with them so quickly was his normal. I really already knew that. I could tell that he was riddled with guilt. I could really make him feel better if I wanted to. I giggled under by breath and wondered how he would feel about me being involved with a married man for years. Oh, and I lived with them both and had a child with him, which they were raising together. Oh yes, that would be a foolproof way of reeling him in. I thought I would just keep that all to myself and let him feel guilty about his actions. It would keep him humble.

The more time I spent with Bo, the more I was starting to realize that I was falling in love with him. It was weird, because although I felt so connected to him, I also felt like I was still more in love with Shawn. How could I still feel this way? Would I ever really get over him? I thought it was time that I shared my feelings with him. Maybe if he knew that I was involved with someone else, he would be so difficult that it would force me to let him go.

Chapter Twenty-Seven

TELLING SHAWN

Shawn hated the thought of me living in California. I was not sure if it was that he really hated the state or he hated that I was not in Oklahoma. I didn't love California, but I loved the ocean and the warm air. The ocean was healing for me, and when I wasn't near it, I felt stressed and a little depressed. I felt like an important part of myself was missing. I thought it was because I grew up and spent most of my life on the East Coast. He said that he didn't understand that. I tried to point out that he loved Oklahoma as much as I loved the coast. He just laughed at me and insisted that Oklahoma was the only place on earth that he would ever be happy.

I knew Shawn would be up bright and early to watch the sunrise. He never missed it. I missed watching the sunrise together. It was so special. It wasn't often that I met a man who appreciated things like the sunrise and the sunset, the color of the sky, and beautiful flowers. He loved them all.

I made myself an americano with three shots of espresso. I knew that I was going to need a little extra courage before I made the dreaded phone call. I went out on the deck and looked out over the water. It was still very dark. I was two hours earlier than him, and I wanted to catch him at sunrise. I picked up the phone and dialed the number.

He picked up on the second ring. It was as if he had the phone in his hand already.

"Hey, baby," he said in the sweetest voice. "I was just thinking about you. I miss you so much."

"I miss you too, Shawn"

Hearing his voice just did something inside of me that I couldn't explain. I felt like my soul had been separated somehow. It was like he had hijacked a piece of my heart that I might never get back. I told him that I had started seeing Bo. As expected, he didn't take the news well at all.

"Taylor, why? Why are you seeing other men? It's killing me inside that you are there and I am here. I can't stand the thought of you being with someone else."

"Shawn, I have to move on with my life. It's not that I don't want you in it. It's just so complicated when you are. I hate myself for letting the rest of the world influence my decision. I love you so much. I know you don't understand, but I need you to try. He is really a great guy."

"Does he know anything about us?"

"No, Shawn! Why would I tell him that?"

"Taylor, we have a child together. I will always be part of your life, and he needs to understand that.

"No, you took our child away! We are not exactly co-parenting, Shawn. We can't start telling people, or the word will be out in the media. I trust Bo, but he can never know the whole story. No one can. He has asked me about my past and I had to lie about everything. I hate that I have to lie to him, but we can't risk anyone knowing, no matter how much we trust them."

"Taylor, hon, I know you're right. I just don't know why we can't be together. Nicole is a mess. She thinks I am the reason that you left. I can't make her understand that it's not my fault. I know why you left. You are weak, and you worry too much about what other people will think or do. I wish you felt that strongly about us. I would sell my soul to the devil himself if I thought that would bring you back to me. I regret the decisions that I have made over the years about my career. I think if I was still Joe Nobody, we would still be together. The American dream is nothing if I don't have you to share it with. I gained everything and lost everything in my life literally overnight.

"My relationship with Nicole since you left has been horrible. She is depressed and is so angry with me. I don't know what I can do to make this right. I can't exactly walk away from the public eye now. That would surely raise a red flag and guarantee that the media would pursue me. I have to try to let you go and see If I can repair my relationship with Nicole. We have to keep our family together for the kids. Especially Preston. I feel he is getting a little suspicious, hearing conversations and fights that Nicole and I have. He is old enough to figure things out if he ever wanted to. I will try to move on with life and accept the fact that you need to be with someone else. It will kill me inside, but I know I need to try. It will be best for us all. Please don't marry him. That would kill me inside. I know that I can sit back and be silent for only so long before I snap. I want you to be happy, but your heart belongs to me. It always will, and nothing will ever change that."

"Shawn, you will always and forever have my heart. Preston is proof of that. I don't know what the future holds for Bo and me, but if you really want me to be happy, then you have to let me go."

Chapter Twenty-Eight

MY MARRIAGE TO BO

Several months passed, and Bo and I were so very much in love. He was so fun to be with. He really was the whole package. He was funny, and so easygoing. We had gained lots of mutual friends as a couple. I still hated the fact that he worked in law enforcement. I worried about him every time he left to go to work. I was getting a little more used to it. Hopefully in time I wouldn't worry as much. His dad was a cop, too. He was very proud of him. Our relationship was getting stronger every day. I was so thankful to have him in my life.

Shawn and I still talked a lot. I hadn't spoken to Nicole since I left Oklahoma. It killed me inside that she had never forgiven me for everything that happened. I thought Shawn was finally at a place in his life where he was finding it easier to let me go. He drank a lot and I did worry about that. I couldn't remember the last conversation we had when he was totally sober. I could always tell when he was drinking because his voice was much lower when he talked—almost a mumble. I saw it in the media too. His biggest critics always commented about him being drunk during a performance. His fans really didn't seem to mind. I think they just found him to be real, someone they could relate to. I just didn't want Preston to think of his dad in a negative way or hear people talk about his dad as a drunk. I tried to talk to him about it, but he just said that he had given up so much already over the years to please other people, and he was not going to give up drinking too.

Bo asked for my hand in marriage. I did love him very much and was excited to spend the rest of my life with him. I decided not to be forthcoming about my past. I still didn't see why he really needed to know about it. I just wanted a clean slate. I was definitely not telling Shawn until after the wedding. I couldn't take the risk of him showing up and showing his ass. Bo knew that my previous relationship took a wrong turn. That was really all he needed to know.

I couldn't say that I was completely over Shawn. I didn't think that I would ever really be over him. I would never cut ties with him, but I had drastically reduced our communication. I wanted so badly to reach out to Nicole. She and I were so close. I wanted her to be part of my life so much. I was hesitant to reach out because I didn't want her to get angry again with Shawn. I frequently saw her from a distance when I secretly visited Oklahoma to spy on Preston. I had attended may of his sporting events and would be attending his high school graduation soon. So far, I had been able to show up unnoticed. I loved seeing him. I wished I could walk up to him and give him a great big hug. I was so proud of him. He was a handsome younger version of his dad.

When I went to Oklahoma, I always hooked up with Shawn. That would need to stop when I married Bo. I wouldn't be unfaithful in a marriage . I was weak, though, when it came to him. I had tried in the past to cut ties completely, without success. I just didn't want to bad enough.

I was busy every day planning a spring wedding. It was getting so stressful trying to please both of our families. Unfortunately, our families didn't share the same religious beliefs. Bo could tell that I was getting frustrated trying to please everyone, so he suggested that we just elope. At first, I was totally against that. I was very close to my family and I really wanted to share this moment with them. The more I thought about it, the more it just made sense. Most of my friends and family were on the East Coast. His family and friends were mostly from the Midwest. Why in the world would we move forward with a big wedding on the West Coast? So, we made the decision to just elope. That was the best decision that we ever made.

We kept out original spring date and married in a secret ceremony in the mountains of upstate New York. We didn't tell anyone until we returned from our honeymoon. It was hard to keep the secret, but we did it. It was beautiful. I wore the same wedding dress that I was going to wear in a big wedding. Our wedding cake was made by Godiva Bakery. It was a perfect way to start our new life. He made me so very happy. For the first time in my life, I was truly happy. My heart still was not totally over Shawn, but I was over him enough to find happiness. I thought so, anyway.

Chapter Twenty Nine

TELLING SHAWN

Almost a year had passed and I still had not told Shawn that Bo and I got married. I was so happy right now, and I just didn't want him to interfere with our life. We talked frequently, but he was so busy on tour that it had been easy for us not to see each other. Preston would be graduating from high school soon, and I planned to attend his graduation. I hadn't decided what I would tell Bo, but I needed to make this trip without him. I hadn't been back to the house Shawn and I built together, but he asked that I stay there while I was in town. He said he would never sell that house. I was excited to see it again. I hoped it didn't cause me to relapse and regret the wonderful and normal turn that my life had taken.

I told Bo that a close family friend's son was graduating from high school and I wanted to go. Fortunately, he was on duty all weekend at work and didn't even express interest in going. A couple of days later, I flew out to Oklahoma . Shawn picked me up at the airport and took me to the house—the house that he built for me. Being there woke up a whirlwind of memories and emotion.

Throughout the house, he had hung various pictures of us. He also had several pictures of Preston. The kitchen was just as I remembered leaving it. I loved being in the kitchen, and I loved to cook. Shawn knew that, and when he built the house for me, he spared no expense designing it.

He took my luggage to the bedroom and waited patiently for me to go in there. When I walked in, he was sitting on the bed. He motioned with two fingers for me to come over and join him. I walked over toward him and he pulled me down onto the bed and started kissing me. I gently pushed him away. I didn't want to, but I did anyway.

"Shawn, I have to tell you something. Bo and I got married."

He sat there without saying a word. His face was emotionless. I thought he would be angry, but he responded more like he was hurt.

"Say something."

"I don't know what to say. You made a promise to me, Taylor, and you broke it. I am just in shock. I never thought you would do this to me."

"Shawn, I had to. I had to move on with the rest of my life."

"What about us, Taylor? Where does this leave us? What about Preston?"

"I will always be here for Preston, whether he knows about me or not. I want to be here for you too, but I need you to understand that I am married now, and our relationship will have to change."

"I don't want it to change. I want things to be the way they have always been. I want us back."

"Shawn, we lost 'us' a long time ago."

I would never forget the look on his face when I told him the news. I knew that I needed to stay strong. We needed to build a new relationship. A relationship with different terms. It took everything in me not to sleep with him . I knew if I did, my relationship with Bo would never be the same. I would be riddled with guilt and I would have to tell him everything. I could never hurt Bo that way.

I took a shower and drove by myself to the graduation. Shawn let me use Nicole's car while I was in town. I was so proud when Preston stood up to receive his diploma. I wanted so badly to run to him. I hoped someday if he found out about me, that he would also know how much I was actually there in his life. I kept a box of pictures of him at various events that I took so someday I could prove to him that I really was there when he was growing up. I was there because I wanted to be there. I did have so many regrets about giving him up. I did what I had to do. I was just in survival mode.

After the graduation, I went back to the house and sat on the back porch. I was hoping deep down that Nicole would come over and join me. Shawn didn't even come back over. I sat out there alone drinking one glass of red wine after another. Nicole and I used to sit on the back porch every night. We talked about everything. I miss her so much.

I forgot how beautiful life was here, but I wouldn't trade my life with Bo for anything in this world.

Chapter Thirty

SHAWN SEEKS REVENGE

Words could not explain how angry and hurt I was when I found out that Taylor got married. I wanted revenge. I wanted them to break up. Deep down, I knew it wasn't the right thing to do, but it was what I wanted to do. I loved her so much, and I couldn't stand the thought of her being married to anyone except me. She should be married to me, not to some random guy who I knew would be incapable of providing for her the way that I could . I hated him for taking her away from me, so I planned to do what I had to do to let him know about me. He needed to know that I would forever be part of her life. I would never let her go.

I sent my best security team to Santa Barbara to gather as much information as they could about this asshole. I got his work schedule and daily routine. I needed that so I could come up with a plan to let him know about me while Taylor believed it was an accident and totally random. She would never forgive me if she thought I planned this. There was not a stitch of my soul that felt bad about doing this. I needed to get her back and I would do whatever I needed to do to make that happen.

After almost a month of spying and gathering information, I was ready to move forward with my plan. I booked a fundraiser for a local children's hospital in Santa Barbara on a Thursday night. That was the night that Bo consistently worked with the police department every week. About a week before the event, I contacted Taylor and told her about it and asked if we could meet. She hesitated a bit, then agreed to meet me but said it needed to be in a public place. She made it clear to me that being intimate was not an option. Meeting in a public place these days was extremely difficult or me. It required a team of people around me at all times. I reluctantly agreed. After all, all I really wanted was for our relationship to be exposed. It didn't really matter how it happened.

After the event we met at a local bar near where she lived. She said that she knew the owner there and that he could offer a more private place to meet. Perfect! I knew a couple of drinks would lead to a couple more drinks. Getting her to drink over the legal limit was part of my plan. We talked and laughed for several hours that night. I wanted to embrace her, but I knew if I wanted this whole thing to work, I needed to play by her rules. She had to think all of this was totally random.

I had one security guy with me that night. I needed him to help pull this whole thing off. It was getting late and she wanted to leave and go get something to eat. I could not let her eat because she hadn't had much to drink, and I needed her to get a DUI with me in the car. It was time to roll, so that's what we did. We got into the car. She put a restaurant into her navigation system, and off we went. Travis waited until we got on the main road and called her tag in to the local police department and reported her as a drunk driver. He told them that he saw her leave the bar and she was weaving all over the road. As we were driving, I started talking dirty to her. I unbuttoned my jeans and grabbed her hand and put it inside my pants. I knew just her touch would cause an erection. Perfect timing. I pulled my pants down a little more to allow her to stroke me, and the blue lights of two different cars were behind us. Perfect!

Taylor was frantic. She immediately pulled the car over. She looked out of the rear view mirror and told me in a panicked voice that it was her husband approaching the car. When he got to the window, he was laughing at her. This was perfect. Maybe she would think that he initially pulled her over for no reason other than to be funny. When he saw me in the passenger's side, things went south fast. Another deputy approached the car. Bo yelled at me and told me to get out of the car. I couldn't do it fast enough, because I wanted him to see my jeans down and my dick hard. Once I stepped out of the car, he asked me who I was. I told him. I purposely used my stage name because I wanted to make sure that he knew who I really was. He was at least a foot shorter than me. His face was red with anger. Bo aggressively lunged at me, so I went for him. Travis got out of the car behind us with his gun in his hand. Once the officers saw Travis with a gun, they both pulled their weapons and they were pointed directly at me instead of him. Taylor yelled over to Travis and told him not to shoot. She told him that it was her husband, and this was all a huge misunderstanding.

Bo arrested Taylor that night and booked her in the county jail with a DUI. Travis and I were also both arrested and charged with assaulting a police officer with a deadly weapon. I didn't even have a gun that night. I have a team of lawyers and security people that take care of me. We were out of the pen within two hours. I tried to bail out Taylor, but for a DUI there was a required 24-hour hold. Bo was furious that Travis and I were released from jail that night, and he knew why. It was because my name carried a lot of status. The next morning while still in a hotel in Santa Barbara, I was watching the local news. There was a breaking story that a police officer who had been on the force for several years had been shot as a result of a drug sting operation gone bad. It was Bo. He had been shot and severely wounded. I felt terrible. I knew that the stress of what happened just two hours before caused him to let his guard down and he didn't react quickly enough. My plan seemed to be perfect until this happened and screwed everything up.

Would Taylor ever forgive me for all of this?

Bo lost two ranks and was put on a desk job as a result of what I did. He also asked Taylor for a divorce. He lost his job and his wife the same night. This wasn't exactly what I wanted to happen. I felt terrible, but sometimes you have to do things out of character to get what you want.

Chapter Thirty-One

IN SEARCH OF ANSWERS

I was beyond devastated about everything that had happened. My heart was shattered into a million pieces. I knew that this was not Shawn's fault, but once again, he had managed to ruin my life. Bo and I were so happy. I knew that I would never find anyone who would love me like he did. I just couldn't seem to wrap my head around what happened. Why was I even pulled over that night? I needed answers. Bo wouldn't even talk to me right now, so I might not know for a long time, if ever. Did he pull me over to be funny? My whole life was spinning out of control. I really wanted to talk to Shawn, but I just couldn't bring myself to do it. Not yet, anyway. I thought I needed to come to the realization that my life would never be normal. Having a baby with Shawn sealed the deal for that. I wished sometimes that I was strong enough to walk away from him. I felt like I couldn't lead a normal life, with him or without him.

MEANWHILE IN OKLAHOMA

I felt truly in the gutter after what happened. It was eating me up that I so selfishly destroyed Taylor's life. I knew that she loved him. She was truly and passionately happy with him and I couldn't stand it. My conscience was killing me, and if I kept drinking like this, I was going to end up in rehab. I had to come clean and tell her what I did. It was eating me up inside. I needed to accept the fact that we might never be together.

"Nicole, I need to talk to you."

"Okay. What's on your mind?"

I couldn't speak a word. Sweat was beading up on my forehead, and I just couldn't get it out. I placed my head in my hands and brushed away the sweat in my hair. I could tell that Nicole was getting upset, so I just started talking. It took me a while to get it all out, but I told her everything. Nicole, true to form, took up for Taylor. She always did, and this time she was right. She was so upset that I hurt her again.

"Shawn, you have to fix this. Have you tried to contact Bo?"

"I tried, but he wouldn't talk to me."

"I don't know how to tell you to fix this, but you need to figure out a way. I think you should call a press conference and come clean with the media. Tell the world everything. I think once it is out there, healing can begin. Taylor has always said that she loves you but she doesn't want your relationship with her to affect your career. I am strong.

You know I can handle the negativity that it will bring. I want Taylor to come back home. Our marriage is at stake here, too. You are not happy, and it is spilling over into our home life. We were both happier when she was here. Preston is in college now. Maybe it's time that we come clean and tell him everything too. I think he is getting suspicious anyway."

"Do you think I should just do it, or should I ask Taylor first?"

"I think you should just do it. In case you haven't noticed, all she has ever wanted to do is protect you. Protect us. She is the most self-less, loving person that I know. Of course she will say don't do it, but trust me when I say this will be the best thing in the long run. She will be upset at first, but when she sees that everything will be okay, she will find relief. If this backfires and your career suffers, then so be it. We have made plenty of money. We live a simple life. But is it really worth it if you lose the woman that you love?

"She makes you happy, Shawn. If you lose her, your life will never feel complete. There will always be a void, that hole in your heart that no matter how hard you try you will never recover from. I am so disappointed at the things that you have done to hurt her over the years. For the life of me I will never understand how you can hurt someone that you love so much. I think that's why you do it. Sometimes being in love makes us do foolish things. I am still so angry with her for leaving. She gave up on us when I needed her the most. Please go and make this right. Think about coming clean to the world. Let's just roll with it and see what happens."

I thought about what Nicole said for a week—a week of excessive drinking and literally no sleep. I made the decision not to tell Taylor but to go to a trusted media source that I knew would cover the story with our dignity intact. I decided to trust Mitchell with the story. It would be a good breaking story for him too. His career could really gain by being the first to report something like this—a story the entire world would be listening to. I knew Taylor would trust him too.

I called him up and ask him to meet with me, and he agreed. We met and had a few drinks and then in a recorded interview I told him everything. Everything except Taylor's name, which I would tell him at the end. He was appreciative of getting to break the story. For a journalist, this was quite a huge deal, and selling his story would mean big bucks for him. He asked me to provide picture proof that my story was true. I brought in three large boxes full of pictures telling the story of our past—over two decades, by this point. I also photocopied songs that I had written about her and various moments in our life. He opened the box and began thumbing through the pictures. As he looked closer, he dropped the pictures that he was looking at and pushed the box away.

"Is this Taylor Ricci?"

I couldn't speak, but my blank stare told the story for me.

"Yes, yes it is. That is why I chose you to cover the story." I knew that you and Lena have been friends with her for years and she would want you to have the story first. I know you must wonder why I am doing this. You see, I have many beautiful years and a lot of memories with this woman. She continues to push me away because of her fear that the media will someday find out and ruin my career. This is my screw the media and the world coming-out party. I need her in my life far more than I need a record label."

"Shawn, as a journalist I need breaks like this to advance my career. Do you realize that I will need to copy some of these pictures and songs? I will need this proof in order to sell the story. The industry will always look at me as the guy that slayed a giant. You are legendary, man, and because of that, and also my deep friendship with Taylor, I am going to need to think about this before I release the story. Will you give me some time to do that? Does Taylor know you are doing this?"

"No, she doesn't, and I need to request that you keep it that way. She would never agree to this, but I don't see any other way to get her back in my life full time. See, if you look through these pictures, you will find a beautiful story of love that spans many years, long before I was anybody. It was my fame that brought this affair down. Look through everything and you will see why I need this to happen. Please let me know if you have any questions. I know this is a big deal and the outcome could go either way. Take as much time as you need to think about it. I want this story to be delivered with care and dignity. That's why I chose you to do it."

BACK IN SANTA BARBARA

I couldn't stand it anymore. I had to confront Bo about why he pulled me over that night. I am pretty sure this would not make a difference in whether or not he divorced me. After all, there was a half-naked man in my car. I just needed to know. I knew he would be getting off of work soon, so I walked down to his house and sat on his porch and waited for him to get home.

Lights flashed over to me as he pulled his car into the driveway. He waited in the car for a bit before he got out. When he did, he just walked right past me sitting on the porch and opened the door and went in. He didn't even acknowledge my existence.

"Bo, please, I really need to talk to you. Please open the door."

He opened the door but left the screen door closed.

"Bo," I said as tears fell down my face. "I really need some answers. Why did you pull me over that night?"

He just stood there emotionless, staring at me.

"Please, I just need to know."

"Your boyfriend called in your tag and said he saw you leave the bar and that you were driving drunk. When I heard the tag number come across the radio, I told the guys that I would handle it since you were my wife. Some boyfriend you have there. He is a real winner. He paid me off to keep my mouth shut. He paid a substantial amount of money to drop the charges against him. How long have you been seeing him?"

"Too long," I said as I just stared at him in disbelief. I was speechless. I couldn't say a word. I just stood there frozen. Bo slammed the door in my face, and I walked home. I could not believe my ears. Did Shawn plan all of this? Was it possible that he purposefully sabotaged my marriage? I stayed up all night long crying. I wanted so badly to confront him. I needed to wait until the time was right. I didn't want to respond in anger.

Chapter Thirty-Two

SEEING PRESTON

*B*lackjack was a college sport for Preston. I would look at the school calendar that was posted online, and frequently I would travel from one location to another to catch a glimpse of him. Seeing him was the only thing that made me happy these days. He was so handsome. I had thought so much about just telling him the truth. I really wanted to be part of his life. I had come to the realization that I would never be able to have a normal relationship or a normal life with another man. I could not risk Shawn destroying another man like he did Bo.

I had often wondered how Preston would respond to the news that I was his mother and that he had been lied to all these years. It could go either way, I guess. I was pretty sure safely say that if I didn't tell him, he would likely never find out.

I was getting older, and I really wanted one more child. I really wanted Shawn to be the father so that Preston would have a full sibling. It was the least he can do for me, since he kept running off every man that I met. I really needed to talk to him anyway, and Preston had a game in Las Vegas, so I asked him to attend with me. So far, I had managed to attend these events completely unnoticed. It would be my first time seeing Shawn since the night that I was arrested. I was a little bit nervous, but I was also kind of excited to be with him again.

We met at a different hotel than Preston was staying at. It would be less likely that we would be caught together that way. Being with Shawn again stirred up a level of emotion that I hadn't felt in a very long time. It felt so good to be in his arms. I asked him if he did in fact make the call to Santa Barbara police to report me drunk to expose our relationship to Bo. He hesitated, but he admitted that he did it. I could tell that he felt terrible about it. I felt terrible that I put him in a situation that he felt like he couldn't live with. I really didn't think he did it to be malicious. I thought he was just so determined for us to be together that he would do anything to make it happen.

We attended all of Preston's games that day. He was a very good player. I watched from a distance, but Shawn sat at the table with him. After the games were over, the boys all went and sat at the bar and had a few drinks. I sat envious across the bar, admiring the close relationship that Shawn had with our son. I noticed that Preston was staring over at me a lot. I began to get a little nervous, so I got up and walked around the bar a few times, and then I found another place to sit and watch them. Later that night, we were ready to retire to our rooms. Once we thought Preston was out of sight, we hooked up and walked to the hotel together.

"Taylor, I don't want you to freak you out or anything. but Preston made a few comments to me tonight that were extremely disturbing. I felt like he was trying to get a response out of me or something."

"What do you mean?"

"Well, he wanted me to look at you sitting across the bar. He said that he found you to be very attractive and that he was into older women. He then proceeded to ask me if I found you attractive. I was so uncomfortable with the whole conversation, and it was as if he was doing it on purpose. He started making comments about your breasts and your ass as you were walking away."

"Oh my God, Shawn!" Do you have that kind of relationship with our son that you talk about sexuality and women with him?"

"No! I do not! I think he was trying to get a reaction out of me!" He even made a comment that he wanted to invite you back to his room. He said more, but I can't bear to discuss it with you."

"I am so weirded out right now, Shawn."

"I think he knows."

"What?"

"I think he knows and he is trying to get me to say something. I could tell that he was trying to upset me on purpose."

"What did you say to him?"

"I didn't know what to say. I told him to go for it!"

"Oh my God! Why would you tell him to do that?"

"What did you want me to say? Should I have told him the truth? I think he already knows. He also told me that he has noticed you hanging around near him. I asked him where, and he said almost all of his gaming events. Nicole also mentioned that she thought he was getting suspicious. I don't know how he would put you in the picture, but I think he has, somehow. He knows that Nicole and I have had problems in the past, but we have always been careful when talking about you."

"Oh, damn, this is getting so complicated. I was really wanting you here with me this weekend so that I could ask you to father another child with me. I really want another baby, but I also want Preston to have a full sibling, but now I'm not so sure. I never thought this secret would ever be exposed."

"Oh, Taylor—I really really would love to have another child with you, a chance to make up for taking Preston away. I love you so much, and I promise you that I will never interfere with your life again. I will let you live in peace, even if you don't want me in your life. I will be here as much or as little as you want me to be. Let's do it! Let's have another baby."

We embraced in a hug and made the decision together that we would have another child. I knew I would never have a relationship with another man, so I was looking at being a single parent, and I was okay with that. With any luck, I would conceive a child before the weekend was over. That was my goal, anyway.

Preston had another game this morning. I tried to stay further away this time, since we thought he might be noticing me. That evening I was sitting at a totally different bar waiting for Shawn to finish up his evening with Preston. The bartender came over and asked to see my ID. I hadn't been carded for years, but I was happy to give it to him. I didn't think much about it at first until I glanced over and I saw the bartender nod his head to someone. I looked over, but it was dark, and I couldn't see who he was nodding to. I was sitting alone drinking my drink when I felt a brush of an arm as someone was getting on the bar stool beside me. I almost fainted. It was Preston.

I wasn't sure if I should walk away or stay. I finished my drink and he offered to buy me another one. I declined, but he motioned for the bartender to bring me one more. He began chatting with me—small talk, really, and honestly, I was so excited to be having a conversation with him. I was talking to my son, and my heart was exploding with happiness. Then, I realized that he called me by my first name. I asked him how he knew my name and he insisted that I introduced myself when he first sat down. I knew that I had not done that. I realized that Shawn was right. He was on to us.

Chapter Thirty-Three

BACK IN SANTA BARBARA

—

$\mathcal{I}$ was late for my period and feeling tired all the time. I was almost certain that I was pregnant. I wanted to wait to tell Shawn until I knew for sure. He was coming here every weekend to see me anyway. I got an over the counter test from the pharmacy and it was positive, so I made a doctor's appointment for the following Monday. I knew that Shawn would want to be there with me. I was so full of excitement. I loved the thought of us having another baby together. I didn't care whether it was a boy or a girl. I just wanted it to be healthy.

Shawn arrived late on Thursday night. I wanted to wait to tell him, but the first thing he did when he arrived was walk over to the bar and fix us both a drink. He brought it over to me and I took both of them out of his hand and asked him to sit down.

"Shawn, I wanted to wait to tell you, but I just can't because I'm too excited. I'm pregnant."

The look on his face was priceless. He grabbed me up and gave me the biggest hug. He lifted me slightly off of the floor and began to whisper seductively in my ear. I loved it when he did that. I always had. It was amazing that after all of these years it just felt right. It still felt very new, and the fire inside of us still burned hot.

"Baby, thank you for giving me another chance to make this right."

"Oh, Shawn, I wouldn't have another child if I couldn't do it with you. I have a doctor's appointment on Monday, and I would love for you to be there with me if you can."

"Baby, I wouldn't miss it for the world."

Our weekend seemed to fly by so fast. I didn't feel like doing much at all. This pregnancy felt very different from my one with Preston. I felt much sicker. I felt nauseated almost all day, and I just didn't have a desire to eat. I had barely started to show, but my feet and hands swelled a lot. We tried to walk a little every day. No matter how bad I felt, we still got up early enough in the morning to watch the sun rise. That memory would always be so special to me.

Monday morning, we showed up at the doctor's office for my first Ob visit. I was so nervous. I hated when they asked me if this was my first pregnancy. I never knew how to answer that question. I was always ashamed to say that it wasn't, for fear that I would be judged. The doctor ordered an ultrasound to get better dates and a good look around. He was certain that I was further along than I thought. I think Shawn was more excited than I was.

"Do you want to know the sex of the baby if we can see?"

Shawn waited for me to answer. I looked over at him and I saw a twinkle in his eyes that I had never seen before and I just blurted out, "Yes! Yes, we do!"

Shawn squeezed my hand in anticipation as the sonographer gently rolled the transducer around on my belly.

"It's a girl!"

We both started to cry. We were having a girl, and we couldn't have been happier.

As we were driving home, I noticed that Shawn was very quiet.

"What's wrong, baby? Why are you so quiet?"

"Taylor, I don't want to leave you here tonight. You don't feel well, and someone needs to be here with you."

"Baby, I will be okay. You can't stop living your life for me. I knew when I decided to do this that it would be just me. I am ready and willing to be a single parent. I will be fine. You need to go back and spend some time with Nicole before you go back on the road. She needs you too."

"Taylor, would you reconsider?"

"Nope, Shawn, just stop right there. I am not coming back to Oklahoma. Please don't get upset, but I need to stay here. My life is here now. Whether you like it or not, California is my home now. I don't want the world to find out about us and judge us. I need you more. I need you to be strong with me right now. As long as we are this far apart, I feel like no one will find out the truth."

"Baby, you are the strongest person that I know. I can't wait to see what our daughter is going to be like."

Shawn left early on Tuesday morning. I really felt terrible. I was vomiting all the time and I felt so weak, but I tried to hide it from him. I know if he thought I was that sick, he would stay. It was more important to me that he go back home and spend time with Nicole. I thought Preston was coming home for a visit this week, and I really wanted him to be there for that.

I was thrilled that I was having a girl. I had been looking all over at girl names. I was not sure if I would give her a family name or come up with a random name that had no meaning. Shawn hadn't mentioned it, but I knew he would like her to have his last name. I had a little bit of time to think about it. If I did that, she and Preston would at least have the same last name. Right now, I was leaning toward that, but I was just not sure.

I wished this morning sickness would go away. Walking outside in the fresh air seemed to help a little. I decided to walk down to the bar and visit with Simon. He was going to die when he saw that I was pregnant. I thought talking with him would be a nice distraction from my extreme nausea.

I walked into the bar and he ran toward me and gave me a great big hug. He noticed right away that I seemed different. I could tell that he didn't want to ask but he definitely thought that I was pregnant. I kept him in suspense for a while before telling him the news. He was ecstatic. He kept asking me questions about who the father was. I didn't want to answer him because I didn't want to lie to him. I didn't notice, but Bo had walked in through a side door and heard our conversation.

He looked over at Simon and blurted out in anger, "His name is Shawn! He is a big country music star asshole. That's the only clue that you are getting from me. I'm not legally allowed to say any more because the bastard dropped me six figures to keep my mouth shut about their relationship. Impressive! Seems like he wants to keep his affair with this little southern belle a secret. Does that make you feel good, Taylor?"

I was starting to get upset, so I just sat there and didn't say a word at first. I started to think about it, and what Bo thought about me did matter. I still loved him and felt terrible about the way things ended with us.

"It's not him, it's me. I am ashamed of being with him because he is married. We have been together since I was seventeen years old. He would tell the world if he could. He hated that we were together, Bo. I never meant to be unfaithful and hurt you that night. You will always be loved by me, no matter how much you push me away. I will always be regretful for losing you. I decided to move on with my life the best way that I knew how, and I'm sorry that you don't approve."

I gave Simon a hug and I walked home that night crying the entire way. I needed to get that all off my chest. It was hard, but it also felt so good.

BACK IN OKLAHOMA

I just came back inside the house and fixed myself a cup of coffee. I went out this morning to watch the sunrise, but it was a little overcast and hardly worth it. As I was walking back to sit on the deck, the doorbell rang. I pulled back the curtain gently to see if I could see who was there. It was Mitchell, and he was holding the boxes in his hand. This could not be good news.

I opened the door and offered him a cup of coffee, and we went on the deck together.

"Shawn, I am sorry, brother, but I can't run this story. I talked it over with Lena and she is furious that you want to do this behind Taylor's back. Lena and Taylor have been friends for many years. I introduced them way before we got married and she has a heightened level of loyalty to her. I have to be honest with you. I could have broken this story years ago. I photographed you and Taylor together making out in the green room before a concert in Charlotte, North Carolina. I have followed you both and secretly documented your private life ever since. I have a photograph of you two having sex in a red Ford truck after shooting a music video in a bar in Tennessee. Lena found out about it and forced me to destroy the pictures. And I did. I destroyed them all.

"My breaking story is not worth losing our friendship with Taylor. I hope that you understand. I have destroyed the interview tape you

130

and I recorded the other day, and as far as I am concerned, I know nothing. Taylor is pretty special. I really urge you to not move forward with exposing your relationship unless she approves of it. If you lose her, you will never get her back. I have known her long enough to know that she doesn't give second chances. Let that sink in, brother. She is worth fighting for, but there has got to be a better way."

LATER IN SANTA BARBARA

I got home and cleaned my face off where I had cried and my makeup ran everywhere. Why did I let Bo upset me so bad? Frankly, none of this was any of his business. I did care about him still, and I hated it that he had such a negative opinion of me. I didn't really cheat on him that night. Shawn made it appear that we did, but we didn't. The truth was, I had never cheated on Bo. I wished I were strong enough to tell him that, but it was obvious that he didn't care to listen. I guess I just loved him more. Someone told me years ago to never love someone more than they love you. At first, I thought that was a terrible rule to live your life by. As I got older, I totally understood it. That's where we get in trouble when we are in love. That was my problem with Bo, and I think that's why it hurt so bad. I did love him more than he loved me. Obviously. I mean, he never really wanted my side of the story.

I heard a soft knock at the door, but it was late and no one ever came to my house. I was afraid to open it, so I just stood in front of it. I heard Bo's voice.

"Taylor, I do still love you. I am broken and I need time to heal. If you have room in your heart for me and want to start over, I am willing to do that. I need you and I am willing to be there for you and your baby. I will step up and be the father that baby needs. I love you with all of my heart, and I always will."

I heard him as he walked off the porch. I peeked out of the window and watched him walk up the road. He didn't really know if I'd heard any of that. I found that very strange. I was so lost right now. I did love Bo, but I could not see myself trying to explain to Shawn that I wanted to raise his baby with someone else.

Chapter Thirty-Four

PRESTON

*L*ife is messy and complicated. I had a great childhood, but at times I just never felt like I really fit in. I started to notice Taylor when I was about fourteen years old. I thought she was pretty and all, but I really started to notice how much she would talk to my dad during my sporting events. She was always there, but I could never connect her to any of my fellow players. I also noticed her taking pictures of me at my high school graduation. Well, I didn't exactly see it at first. It was my overly jealous girlfriend at the time that spotted her and accused me of having an affair with her. That was my sign that I needed to dump this girl. And I did. So I am thankful for that wake-up call.

The funny thing is, I never connected her to my mom's friend that used to live with us when I was very young. I have no memory of that. actually. Once I headed off to college I started playing two sports. Golf and blackjack . Funny that this mystery women apparently had an interest in both. As did my dad. So…it was only natural that I connected the dots and the light came on and I figured it out. I thought I did, anyway. Dad must be having an affair with this woman. Right? That would solve the mystery as to why I saw her so much. No. That didn't exactly add up either. I had two older sisters. I asked them both if they had ever seen her at any of their school events—sporting events or graduations. They both acted really weird about it but denied knowing her. My middle sister said she looked a lot like my mom's friend, the one who used to live with us. They were both old enough to remember. I couldn't wrap my head around any of this. She also said she thought she remembered her being pregnant, but she couldn't confirm that with certainty.

The more I tried to figure this whole thing out, the more odd and complicated it seemed to get. I finally just decided that she was having an affair with my dad. Perhaps my events were just an excuse for my dad to get away, and seeing her there was just a bonus. I kind of wrote off what my sister had told me about her being Mom's friend. If she were Mom's friend, I think I would have remembered her.

During my first year of college, I met a wonderful girl who I knew would end up being the one. She was amazing in every way. We did everything together. She loved to golf, and we often played in our spare time. I brought this whole thing up to her and I even pointed Taylor out to her at several events of mine. She told me this whole suspicion was unwarranted. It was just an odd coincidence that I kept seeing her. I really convinced myself that she was right. I was getting consumed with everything, and I decided that it was time to just let it go—write it off and never think about it again.

I spent Christmas with her family this year. I was ready to ask her to marry me, and I thought it would be important that her family meet me first. On Christmas morning, we all gathered around the tree and each opened a gift one by one. She gifted me one of those DNA kits that everyone was doing. I thought it was a very odd gift, but I would never want to hurt her feelings, so I just acted excited about it. I always wondered if I had any Native American in my blood, so it was gonna be kind of fun to do it.

I waited a couple of weeks after Christmas and I finally sent it in. The funny thing was when I mentioned it to Mom and Dad, they both acted really strange about me doing it. I didn't think much about that.

They were my parents. They always acted weird.

Over the years, I have tried to get Dad to admit to me that he was having an affair with her. I never asked directly, but I once told him I was interested in pursuing her just to get his reaction. I told him one time that there was something about her the made me want to pull her hair and slap her ass. Still, no reaction. He totally denied knowing her.

I was in class one day when I got a notification on my phone that my DNA report was ready. I was excited to check it out. To my surprise, I had no Native American Indian in me at all. This was a total shock. Mom's grandfather was born and raised on a reservation in Wyoming. We thought so, anyway. Later that night my girlfriend and I were sitting on the sofa playing video games and I got another notification. It read: "You have new DNA relatives." I clicked on it, and several people came up—first and second cousins, a few names that I recognized but several first cousins that I did not. I scrolled up to the top and there it was. The notification that would change my life forever. Taylor Ricci, biological mother. I couldn't believe what I was reading. I had no idea what Taylor's last name was, but I needed to find out tonight. I racked my brain to try and remember. I knew I needed to call my dad, and I needed him to tell me the truth.

It was well after midnight, but I had to make the call. Dad answered, and I could tell that he had been drinking and he was quite possibly drunk.

"Hey, Dad, It's Preston."

"Hey, son," he said with a slurred tone. "Is everything okay?"

"Hey, Dad, that girl that I pointed out to you at the bar, Taylor. Do you know her last name?"

"Yes, Ricci. Why do you ask?"

I sat there silent. Speechless. I could tell that Dad immediately regretted saying it, but he couldn't back out of it now. I dropped the phone in complete disbelief. I didn't even bother to hang it up. I just dropped it and walked away.

I was right. My suspicions all of these years had been right. I mean, I never thought in a million years that she was my mother, but I was spot on with the affair. It hit me like a ton of bricks. This was no new affair. It had to date back well over twenty years ago. I started to feel sick to my stomach. Should I let this go and let it remain a secret, or should I expose the truth? I couldn't believe that Mom and Dad both had lied to me all of these years.

I had a blackjack tournament in Las Vegas this weekend and it was highly likely that she would surface at some point. I just needed to see her face one more time before I made a decision as to whether or not to confront her. Until then, I decided I would keep all of this to myself. I didn't want to many people to know.

I was at the tournament less than an hour when I noticed her sitting alone in the corner of the bar. She had a bottle of water in her hand and what looked like a carrot. I found that so odd. A carrot? Who in the hell eats a carrot in a bar? I walked over toward her and was going to take the stool next to her. I didn't know what my plan was. I just wanted to be near her. She noticed that I was walking over, and she quickly got off of the bar stool and walked away. As I got closer, I noticed that she appeared to be pregnant. Pregnant? Could this be right? Could she be pregnant? It was not an if. She definitely was. She was wearing a crop top and a pair of shorts. Her belly was slightly showing, and it was no doubt a baby bump. I could also tell by the slight waddle in her walk. I could absolutely not confront her while she was pregnant.

Just being around her made my heart race. This explained so many things in my life. Her whole family seemed to be listed on the DNA list. Maybe this was their Christmas gift last year to one another. I laughed at the thought, but I was shattered inside. I wasn't quite sure how to feel or react. I knew that I had a grandfather and a great-grandfather that were still alive. I wanted to know them. It appeared that the family was also very large.

I talked to Dad after losing my tournament. I knew I didn't stand a chance of winning. Not today, anyway. I was way too stressed. I didn't think Dad even remembered my call.

A YEAR LATER

*M*ore than a year had passed now, and I still hadn't told anyone my news. I was getting married next week in Mexico and a part of me wanted to ask her to be there. Another part of me kinda felt like she would be there anyway. Incognito, somewhere in a corner. I struggled every day with all of this. My fiancée thought I should reach out to her, but I didn't want to hurt my mom. She raised me, so she was really my mother. I just wished I knew all of the circumstances. It seemed so odd that my dad might still be seeing her. I thought I would just wait it out. I made the decision to confront her if she did in fact show up at the wedding.

During the wedding, I looked all over for her. It wasn't until the reception that I spotted her. I had to walk back out to the beach where the wedding was performed, because I left my cell phone there. It was dusk, but I saw two people sitting in the chairs. As I got closer, I saw them in plain sight. They were holding hands sitting in the same chairs my wedding guests had been in just an hour earlier. My dad, who had not noticed me yet, leaned over to kiss her. They embraced in a kiss and I just stopped and stood there, staring at them both. I was in complete shock. Taylor looked over at me and then motioned something to Dad. He turned back and looked at me. I could tell he was freaking out inside. Taylor got up and started to walk away. I was frozen and couldn't move. Dad walked over to me and I just motioned for him to stop. I couldn't do this today. I grabbed my phone and I walked away.

I didn't see Dad the rest of the night. I went out early the next morning because I knew that he would be out watching the sunrise. He never missed it. It was a beautiful warm morning. As I walked a little farther down the beach, I could see Dad in the distance, and she was with him. I watched them for a while. I couldn't believe the laughter. They were running around chasing each other, and I couldn't remember the last time I saw Dad so happy.

I realized that morning that I needed to just let this all go. If I brought all of this to light, a lot of people would be hurt. I knew Mom and Dad loved me and raised me the best they could. I also knew that Taylor also cared about me, because she was always there—in secret, but there. I couldn't figure out the circumstances surrounding this whole thing, but what I did know was that she made Dad very happy. Dad and Mom seemed to still be happy, and I was happy. For me, that was enough.

BECAUSE THERE ARE TWO SIDES TO EVERY STORY

—————

SHAWN:

*A*fter only a couple of days of planning, Taylor left Oklahoma in the middle of the night. It took everything in me to move forward. I was truly broken. My heart was broken. My spirit was broken and my soul was broken. I would never recover from the emptiness that I felt inside. We truly shared a beautiful bond. We loved to watch the sunrise together, and we never missed a chance of doing so. It didn't matter how tired we were. Every morning I woke up with her, we watched the sunrise. It was our precious thing we had together. The sunrise was a symbol of a new day. A new beginning.

The problem with the beginning....

I admit from the beginning it was I who started everything off on the wrong foot. First of all, Taylor was seventeen years old when we met. She was a minor. I was twenty-seven years old, married, and had two children. Up until that point, I had never even thought about being unfaithful to my wife. It was almost a year later that I discovered her age. It never occurred to me to ask her. We met in a bar. I just assumed that she was at least twenty-one. Taylor was wise beyond her years, so very smart and mature—nothing like you would expect a seventeen-year-old girl to act. I fell in love with her almost immediately. She made eye contact with me and it was hypnotic. I felt like our souls were forever connected.

I would visit her when she was in college, often taking her away for my own selfish reasons, knowing she needed to focus on school. She admitted to me that her grades were suffering because she was missing so much class, yet I continued to do it. Again, I know it was so selfish of me. I also know for this reason, and her taking time off to have Preston, that she changed her major and dropped out of medical school. I have and will continue to compensate her well for this. I am so deeply regretful for the role that I may have played in the precious future that was destroyed possibly because of me.

Her family hated me. Not because they knew me—they in fact knew very little about me. At the time, I was lower to barely middle class. I grew up on a farm with very little means. My brother committed suicide as a result of years of drug and alcohol abuse. Basically, I wasn't, at least at the time that we met, good enough for their daughter. Her dad threatened to kill me, and her brother actually tried to kill me years later. But you get the picture. This poor to middle class country boy was not good enough for their daughter born into great means and family money.

It was never about money with Taylor. In fact, when we met I couldn't afford to buy my own beer when we went out. She often paid for everything. What we had was real. In fact, sometimes I really feel deep down inside that had I not finally made it big, I would still have her in my life. I really feel regretful some days. Did I trade my soul and heart for money and greed? She was just happy being in love. A heart of gold. She and Nicole made life so good for me over the years. I really don't deserve either one of them.

My biggest regret—well, I have two, but I will start with the first one. It was the night that I hit her. That is not who I am. I would never hit a woman. Anger just hit me, and I snapped. I had no control of it. Seeing her almost naked collecting money for a lap dance just set something off inside of me. I have a whole different view when I watch shows like *Snapped* and *Court TV*. It really does happen. When that something inside you snaps, you are powerless to do the right thing. My second and biggest regret was forcing her to give up Preston. She really sugarcoats the truth. The truth is that I threatened her. I was big, a celebrity with endless means to fight her. I was an asshole. I was a terrible father, too. I was never home. Nicole was an amazing mother, but Taylor deserved to be with her son. I have tried to make this up to her over the years, but as you know, especially if you are a mother, there is no way to make up for that. Taking a child away is hateful and a horrible thing to do to someone. I didn't do it to be revengeful because she was leaving me; I did it because deep down I wanted a son. I wanted him to be my legacy when I am gone. I wanted my name to continue on. Basically, I did it for all the wrong reasons. Taylor really wanted another child. She wanted Preston to have a full sibling. I agreed, and a couple of years later we had a daughter together. Now, I have had to watch her grow up from afar—a secret child only Nicole and I know about. She will never be my legacy. She does not even share my last name. I love her so much. I know my blood runs through her, and that will have to be enough. For now, anyway.

I am also deeply sorry for destroying her relationship with Bo. All she wanted to do was have a normal life with someone to love her. I purposely and maliciously destroyed them both. I tried to extend my apologies and regret over the years to him, but he has had no interest in repairing things with me, and I don't blame him. Losing Taylor is not worth any amount of money I could offer him. I have been told that over the years he has never been able to maintain a normal relationship with anyone because of trust issues caused by me. Taylor never slept with me after she and Bo got married. I will forever be sorry for messing up this young man's life. I wish that he knew how loyal and honest she was with him. I vowed and promised to never

ever tell another soul about our relationship. To this day, I can look anyone square in the eye and totally deny knowing her. I need her in my life more than I need people knowing about it.

I will always love Taylor. I will forever be thankful for my family with her and Nicole. I will never ever give up on her. She promised to marry me someday before I die, and I hope that she does. I still watch the sunrise every morning. Taylor and I still, after all of these years, share a special bond. I don't know how she stays so strong. I admit that I drink a lot. I have tried to stop over the years, but I just don't want to bad enough, I guess. I drink because it numbs the heartbreak. I don't get to see her nearly as often as I'd like. She is content still living on the coast of California. I will never understand that.

Every night I pray that she will come back to me, and with every sunrise I have hope.

I will never give up on us.

Forever yours and forever in love,

Shawn

TAYLOR

After a few short days of planning, I did leave Oklahoma in the middle of the night. I had to. Donna really made me realize that if we let our guard down, we would fool no one. I couldn't take a chance of hurting Shawn's career that he worked so hard to get. I had to do it to protect everyone. Believe me when I say that it was one of the hardest things I have ever had to do. Nicole was like a sister to me. I loved her so much. It hurt almost more leaving her than it did leaving Shawn. We had developed such a unique bond that no one will or can really understand. It was so hard walking out that night. I never really said goodbye to Preston. I told him I was moving away for a while, but he really didn't understand that I would never be back.

Shawn and I did start off on the wrong foot. The age difference was never an issue for me. I was seventeen but I had graduated early from high school and was already in college. I was mature enough—or so I thought, anyway. I will never forget the night that we met. The next two nights were life-changing for me. I fell in love with him almost instantly, and no matter how many years have passed and how many problems we have had, I am still madly in love with him.

We had so many obstacles to overcome. My family, especially my dad, hated him. It is sad, but it is true that they hated him because they thought he wasn't good enough for me. He came from a lower to middle class family and they didn't want me to ever be part of that.

They did not know about our age difference or him being married. It was pure prejudice, because he wasn't enough like me.

I will always love Shawn, and nothing will ever change that. He is a kind and gentle man. I wish we had met under different circumstances. I will forever be thankful for Preston. I will never know if I did the right thing by letting Shawn and Nicole raise him, but I did what I thought was the right thing at the time. I will always be his mother, and that will need to be enough.

I am so thankful for our daughter. I see so much of him in her. See, Shawn thinks that just because we hide her identity from the world and she doesn't share his last name, that she will not be his legacy. I strongly disagree. As young as she is, she already is so much like him. His blood runs thick in her. I want her to make her own way. I never wanted her to ride the wave on his coattails. The world will know her someday. She is a natural-born performer and has been for years. It was important to me that she have the same father as Preston. I wanted them both to know that they were never thought of as a mistake. Preston was not planned, but fate had a different plan for us.

Nicole, I will forever be thankful for you. I love you so much. The world that we live in is so caught up on the negativity of infidelity, but you taught me an important lesson in life. You taught me that it is possible to be in love with two people. Love chose us to be a family, and you played such an important role in keeping us all together. See, Nicole never tried to tear us apart. She never made me feel bad or uncomfortable with the choices that Shawn and I made. She made us both understand that we were not totally wrong as long as we loved each other as one family. One unit. Our children were our children. No steps and no halves. It was our family. I bet you are thinking she did this all because she didn't want to lose the money now that Shawn had made it big. Wrong. When we all first met, he was broke as shit with zero possibilities in sight. She truly wanted everyone to be happy. She knew that leaving Shawn would be harder than knowing about me.

That tells you what an incredible man he is.

Nicole has spoken to me very little over the past years since I left. I understand that I hurt her, but I hope that she realizes that I left a part of me there that night that I will never be able to replace. I've had countless failed relationships because I just can't replace what I used to have. We are talking more now and really trying to get to know each other again. I hope we can someday mend our broken hearts and move forward in our lives together. I love you, Nicole. I always will. I will always be thankful for the role that you played in Preston's life.

I have promised to marry Shawn someday. I will keep that promise. Until then, every sunrise will bring me hope and the promise of a new day.

I will never give up on us, and I will forever love you,
Taylor

NICOLE

*I*nfidelity is one of the most negative words in a marriage. Just because you are married, does that really mean you can't ever love someone else? We really need to overcome the stigma that all marriages need to be monogamous. It's not always natural. For us, blending our families felt right. Sure, I was hurt and devastated at first, but I knew my husband, and I knew how wonderful he was. If he made the choice to fall in love with someone else, it had to be an exceptional situation. An exceptional person. I realized that I didn't want to walk away from him. I wanted to walk forward with them both. It really worked for us. Taylor was amazing, and I fell in love with her before I really knew her. She was like a sister to me. Shawn was very respectful around the two of us, and that forged a stronger bond. He never made us feel like he loved one of us more than the other.

You see how both of our situations were handled so differently and they have drastically different outcomes. Bo responded very negatively when he thought Taylor was unfaithful. It destroyed their loving relationship and left them both incapable of maintaining a normal life. Sadly, sweet Taylor had never even cheated on him. Yes, she still maintained a relationship with the father of her child, but she also made it very clear that their relationship had to change. She couldn't tell him about Preston; she had to protect her son. That's what mothers do, right or wrong. When I found out about Shawn's infidelity, yes, my first response was that I wanted to leave him. After thinking about it and knowing that I didn't want to live without him, I decided to have an open mind and just roll with it. Either their relationship would end, or we could all live happily together. I played along to see what would happen. It ended up being so beautiful. Our relationship was better together. See, we all need to have an open mind and think about things and not be so quick to throw it all away. Love is a beautiful thing. We should embrace it.

I was ready to tell the world years ago about our unconventional arrangement. Maybe we could set an example for other couples that may be struggling in this same situation. I didn't because Taylor wanted it to be private. I hope someday we can bring our family back together. She still has an active, loving relationship with Shawn. She never had to stay with him. He has compensated her dearly over the years. She doesn't stay for the money. She truly and deeply loves him, and he is madly in love with her too. I look forward to the day we can be a family again.

Every summer night when I sit outside on my porch alone with a glass of wine, I see tons of fireflies. They have always reminded me of my sweet Taylor—so bright and courageous. I will forever love you, and my heart will not be the same until you come back home to Oklahoma.

Love,
Nicole

THE END FOR NOW

Coming 2020

Because of You:

Chasing Santa Barbara

After Preston saw Shawn and me that night in Mexico, my life had never been the same. As far as we both knew, he never told anyone anything. From that day forward, my motherly instinct just wanted to protect my son. I knew that when he was ready, he would come to me. Until then, I would stay as far away as possible.

Shawn and I had a beautiful daughter and now it was his turn to face the pain of having a child and be unable to be an active part of her life. He spent a lot of time in Santa Barbara lurking in the shadows and being in the background as much as possible. I did not give her his last name. I felt like I needed to try one more time to forge a relationship with someone who could be a father to her and a soul provider for me. I chose to try again with Bo. Actually, I was very much in love with him, and through hours and hours of counseling I knew he realized that what we had was worth fighting for. I never cheated on him. The whole thing was a huge misunderstanding. It wasn't that I thought that Shawn would not be a great father, but until he retired, I still couldn't bear the backlash society would dish out to us if they knew our story. We had a loving, committed relationship and we both now knew that it was best hidden in the darkness—for now, anyway.

Nicole and I were moving forward to repair our relationship. She had always been so supportive of every aspect of my life. Determined to keep our families together, our bond would strengthen to a level that most people would never be able to understand. What happened during the next few years as our daughter grew up will tap into your every emotion.

This book will hopefully change your mind about how we define marriage and family. Love is a strong force. We need not be so quick to throw it all away. I will never feel complete until our family is back together.

ACKNOWLEDGMENTS:

My deepest thanks goes to my husband, who despite my shenanigans has always been my biggest fan. His love and support made my dreams a reality.

To my two college roommates, though they both rest in peace, my heartiest of thanks. K&D taught me to never save champagne to celebrate because we should celebrate every day with champagne. Life taught me to never take my friends for granted, because these two angels left me far too soon.

To Kim, Susan, Rocio, Rhonda, Michelle, Michele, Grace, Shelley and countless others I am truly grateful for your invaluable friendship. You have all carried me through the hardest moments of my life. I will be forever thankful. Cassidy, You taught me to believe in fate and that everything happens for a reason #ChasingColorado, you will always hold a special place in my heart. A personal thanks to Kimberly Ayers for keeping me afloat and assuring me that I would not die this year. Life would suck without you.

Saving the best for last.... A special thanks to Jennifer Cooper-Foreman who is to credit for my happiness today. I had to work hard to win her over as a friend but I now have a loyal friend for life. Thank you for your valuable input while writing this book.

For all of my friends and family I am truly grateful.

CPSIA information can be obtained
at www.ICGtesting.com
Printed in the USA
FSHW022125170820
73000FS